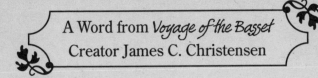

A Word from *Voyage of the Basset* Creator James C. Christensen

Years ago, while watching a documentary about Charles Darwin, I realized that something very important had been overlooked on HMS *Beagle*'s historic voyage. I thought to myself, What if someone had sailed in the opposite direction? Not toward science, but toward *imagination*. That was the beginning of *Voyage of the Basset,* a book I wrote and illustrated over a four-year period, and which was published in 1996.

In the book, a professor of mythology and his two daughters, Miranda and Cassandra, board a magical vessel, HMS *Basset*. During their journey, the family visit the court of the fairies, fight loathsome trolls, and discover the secret of the unicorn. Ultimately, they learn how vitally important the imagination is to the human spirit.

Just as the imagination is limitless, so too are the continuing adventures of HMS *Basset!* Some of my favorite authors have signed on to explore new ths and important new truths. The tides with us—shall we board?

VOYAGE OF THE BASSET

ISLANDS IN THE SKY

BY TANITH LEE

Random House ⌂ New York

Copyright © 1999 by James C. Christensen and The Greenwich Work-
shop®, Inc. All rights reserved under International and Pan-American
Copyright Conventions. Published in the United States by Random
House, Inc., New York, and simultaneously in Canada by Random House
of Canada Limited, Toronto. Based on *Voyage of the Basset* by James C.
Christensen, a Greenwich Workshop book published by Artisan, 1996,
and licensed by The Greenwich Workshop®, Inc.

www.randomhouse.com/kids

Library of Congress Cataloging-in-Publication Data:
Lee, Tanith.
Islands in the sky / by Tanith Lee.
p.   cm. — (Voyage of the Basset ; #1)
"Based on Voyage of the Basset by James C. Christensen"—T.p. verso.
Summary: While climbing a tree to rescue a kite, eleven-year-old Hope is
pulled into the sky, away from the reality of life in London in 1867, and
into a world of magic.
ISBN: 0-679-89127-7 (pbk.)
[1. Fantasy. 2. Magic—Fiction.] I. Title. II. Series: Lee, Tanith.
Voyage of the Basset ; #1.
PZ7.L5149Is 1999 [Fic]—dc21 99-23981
Printed in the United States of America 10 9 8 7 6 5 4 3 2 1

RANDOM HOUSE and colophon are registered trademarks
of Random House, Inc.

Cover illustration by Greg and Tim Hildebrandt.

CONTENTS

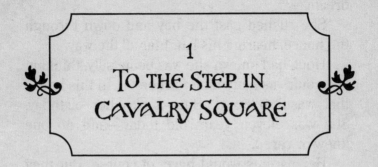

1
TO THE STEP IN CAVALRY SQUARE

One spring morning in 1867, Hope Glover was being an Arabian princess in a corner of the attic. She had just stepped from a flying carpet, and in the early sunlight, the attic had become the top of a golden tower.

"I have returned, my people," cried Hope (sure she was quite alone), "after seven years, to tell you all the wonders I have seen." She flung out one graceful hand, widened her eyes—and saw the horrible footman, who was fourteen, sneering in the doorway. She hadn't been alone after all.

"You've got a nerve," said the footman. "Think you're a great actress, do you? Well, they want you downstairs, in the kitchen."

Hope was both ashamed and scared. Never

before had anyone caught her acting out a day-dream—

She rushed past the boy and down through the house, hearing his laughter all the way.

Hope had known she was being silly, thinking she could take any time for herself. In this house that wasn't allowed. But—it was her birthday. She was eleven years old today—and no one knew or cared.

Her parents would have, of course. But they had died when she was very young. Although the aunt who had brought Hope up had told her she would do better *not* to remember them, Hope did remember. Her parents had been wonderful, and Hope's mother had told her wonderful stories—from Greek myths, from the *Arabian Nights*—

All Hope had left of her parents was their memory, and the stories, and a pair of rainbow-colored gloves, which her mother had knitted for her when she was only two or three. The gloves were now too small for her to wear, but she kept them in her box in the attic where she slept. Sometimes she heard her mother's remembered voice: "I hope these gloves will fit Hope Glover!" But when Hope thought of this, she always wanted to cry.

This big smart house where Hope now lived—Number 15, Cavalry Square—stood amid many more big smart houses, and in the center of the square was a public garden. Today the sun sparkled and birds sang in the tall trees, while all around lay the great city of London, with bells ringing and the sound of cart wheels on cobbles.

Hope's aunt, who had always worn purple and was always slapping her, had said Hope was lucky to get a place as a maid in this fine house. "You can't," declared the aunt, "live in Cloud-Cuckoo-Land. Even if your head's always in the clouds! Pull yourself together," added the nasty woman.

Hope had come to the house last year. It belonged to Mr. and Mrs. Rivers.

"Idle wretch, worth less than this cabbage!" yapped Mrs. Crackle the cook as Hope entered the kitchen.

Hope *hadn't* been idle. She had been up, as usual, since dawn. She seldom got to bed, either, before ten at night. All day long she worked, scrubbing floors or pans, cleaning fireplaces or laying fires, running errands, carrying things. If she stopped still for more than two minutes someone would pinch her or shout. The cook was the worst.

Mrs. Crackle was a vast woman who would have made the huge hateful aunt look quite small.

"Lazy flouncy pest!" the cook thundered, and got ready to throw something at Hope. Generally the thrown thing was fairly soft—a greasy washrag or stale muffin—but this morning it was a saucepan, and Hope only just ducked in time.

Mrs. Crackle had a Bad Temper (with capitals). She was constantly boasting of it herself, as if proud of being a disgusting person.

All the servants, though, were humble before Mr. and Mrs. Rivers. Always going grandly in and out, the master and mistress swept up and down the house. Not often had they spoken to Hope.

Today their son was coming home for a holiday from his school. Hope and Apollo Rivers had met on his last holiday, at Christmas. If you could call it a meeting.

Apollo had ordered her about, and been very unpleasant, calling Hope a "slave," and announcing that he was going to be "important" when he grew up. Suddenly Hope had heard herself telling him he would be a rude idiot when he grew up, just as he was now. The moment after she said it she'd turned white with fear and fled; she still had reason to believe he might have a score to settle with her.

But right now there was Mrs. Crackle.

"Pick up that pan—wretched pest to make me throw it at her! Work-shy, the lot of you!" bellowed Mrs. Crackle.

"She was upstairs acting," said the footman.

Hope wished she could vanish in a puff of smoke as the magician had in her daydream. Then she realized the footman was looking at her in an odd way—almost as if he were impressed. But that couldn't be the case, of course.

And, "Acting? *Acting?*" bawled the cook, "*I* could act if I had the time! *Act?* What is she here for, the little monster?"

Someone pushed Hope. "Go on, you. Go and see to the step!"

Relieved to escape, yet Hope's heart sank. Now she was running through the house, to the front step, to try to scrub it, which was an impossible task. It would never come clean.

"You be thankful, my girl!" someone called after Hope. "You should be grateful."

Hope wasn't.

However, ten minutes later, she was kneeling on the step, her long hair wisping out from under the ugly maid's cap, *scrubbing*.

And, as always, unlike all the other gleaming front steps in the square, this one wasn't gleaming, *wouldn't* gleam.

Hope scrubbed and scrubbed, flushed now, her birthday forgotten, and growling under her breath, "Urrh! Rhrrrrr!"

A passing dog on a lead glanced at her uneasily. The lady and gentleman walking it also glanced at Hope. Then stopped.

Now there would be more trouble, of course.

"I think this is the house," said the gentleman. "And look, there's a *Hyacinthus herbae* growing by the gate."

"Yes, dear," said the lady. "That's very nice. Down, Zeus," she added to the dog, which had suddenly sprung the length of his long lead at Hope. "It's all right, he's very gentle, only friendly. I don't know what breed he is. He followed me home one night in Greece, so I thought I should keep him."

Hope wasn't sure if the lady meant the dog, who now had his paws on her shoulders, or the gentleman, who was craning interestedly with a magnifying glass over a blue weed by the gate.

Then the dog let Hope go. She stroked his head and saw that 1) he had left dirty paw marks on the step, 2) he'd upset the pail, and 3) the lady, who had the brightest golden hair, was standing as still as if she had been suddenly changed to stone, staring and staring into Hope's face.

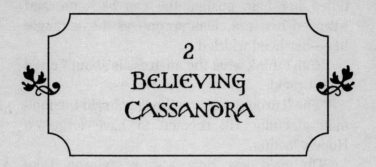

2
BELIEVING
CASSANDRA

The Riverses' butler showed the lady and gentleman (and their dog) into Mrs. Rivers's sitting room. By then Hope had been shooed away back belowstairs to the kitchen.

Here, Mrs. Crackle threw a piece of toast at her, and the footman explained how Hope had made the front step worse, spilling her pail on it and leaving dirty marks. Hope felt herself going red with anger, frustration, and fright, but just then another of the maids put her head around the door.

"Special visitors, Mrs. Crackle. China tea and best biscuits and cake on a tray. And *she's* to serve it."

"She? *Who?*"

The maid pointed sneeringly at Hope.

No one was more astonished than Hope. As

they grabbed her, pulled off her cap and painfully tidied her hair, pushed the cap back on, and wrapped her in a clean apron—as if to strangle her—her head whirled.

"Can't think what the mistress is about," cried Mrs. Crackle.

"She'll drop the tea on the lady," said the footman gleefully. He seemed to have forgotten Hope's "acting."

The maid gave Hope a shove. "Go on. Take the tray. And don't *dare* spill it."

Hope went upstairs. The butler, with a hateful glower, let her into the sitting room.

There sat Mrs. Rivers, smiling like a crocodile at the golden-haired lady. The gentleman and dog weren't there.

Hope set down the tea things.

"*Where* is the sugar?" asked Mrs. Rivers, now a crocodile that glared.

Hope felt panic rising.

"Oh, but Mrs. Rivers," said the golden-haired lady, "no one at *all* takes sugar now, in fashionable circles."

"They don't?"

"Oh, *no,* indeed not. How very clever of your maid to know not to bring it."

Only Hope seemed doubtful of the truth of this. But just then there was a loud crash, and barking, elsewhere in the house.

Mrs. Rivers rose. "My husband—"

"Yes, of course, do go and see," said the lady with golden hair. "I'm afraid *my* husband is so careless—"

Looking very worried, Mrs. Rivers fled heavily out of the room. Hope gazed after her. She had never seen Mrs. Rivers move so fast.

"Hope?" said the young lady. "That was what she said you were called, am I right? Good. Now come and sit here and help me eat these cakes."

"I'm not allowed—"

"Yes, you are. Come on, quick. Before that awful dragon comes back!"

The next moment Hope found herself sitting on the sofa beside the golden lady, who was handing her a plate with three cakes on it.

Hope took the plate and sat stupidly, looking at it.

The lady sipped her tea. She said, "My name's Cassandra. If you're wondering what that crash was, my husband, Edmund, who is a darling and brilliant, but quite mad, has just accidentally dropped Mr. Rivers's biggest glass case of moths."

Hope opened her mouth, then shut it. Mr. Rivers collected dead butterflies and moths, along with other unpleasant things, and put them in glass cases, where he seemed to think they looked nicer than when flying around. Which they didn't.

"Of course," said golden Cassandra, "I asked Edmund to do it—he's such a dear! Then he'll have trodden in the broken case and had a pretend sneezing-and-or-fainting attack because of the nasty stuff the poor moths were dried in. That should keep everyone busy for at least ten minutes.

"We *did,*" she added, "come to see if Mr. Rivers would help fund our next expedition to the tropics. But never mind. Probably Mr. Rivers would have wanted Edmund to dig up lots of plants to give him, dead preferably, like the moths. And Edmund wouldn't have agreed. Someone will fund us, I'm sure. Edmund is quite a famous botanist."

Hope felt she couldn't speak. She swallowed and felt she could.

"Why?"

"Because he's so clever—oh, you mean why did he drop the case. For the same reason I asked if you would serve the tea. I wanted to talk to you in private." Cassandra smiled. "Do eat some cake, then I can eat mine."

Hope ate a cake. She couldn't taste it. Did adults really behave like this? she wondered. It seemed to Hope her own parents had been just this way, young and full of fun, adventurous and—well, a little crazy. But her aunt would have said, "What rubbish. How can you remember?"

Besides, why would Cassandra want to talk to, of all people, Hope?

"A few years ago—actually, *several* years ago—" said Cassandra, "I went to a wonderful place. It was a sort of school. Only school sounds dull, and this was anything but. It was called the College of Magical Knowledge."

Hope said, before she could stop herself, "What a good name!"

"Isn't it? There's a Keeper of Questions there, and he played a sort of game. That is, he asked us questions, rather than answer the questions we'd come to ask *him*. And do you know, because of all the questions *he* asked, we—or my father—found the answer we wanted."

"Yes?" Hope said doubtfully. In her experience people didn't often ask questions, they *told* you things. Go here, do that, be quiet, be grateful, behave yourself, don't *ever* dream. This harsh and boring and hopeless place, this is the *real* world.

As she considered this, Hope saw Cassandra's large eyes resting on her thoughtfully.

"Let's play the question game, Hope."

"What do I do?"

"Let me ask you a question."

"All right."

"What would you like most in the world?"

Hope felt a sort of rush of light go through her. She almost tried to say what she wanted. But then everything she'd ever been told came and stopped her. She didn't know. So little was possible.

Sullenly, she said, "Well, I won't get it, will I?"

"Why not, Hope?"

"Because they'll make sure I can't."

"Who will?"

"*All* of them. Mrs. Crackle, and the Riverses, and horrible Master Apollo—"

"Apollo!" exclaimed Cassandra. Then she checked herself. "Who is Apollo? Apart from the sun god in mythology…"

"Oh, he isn't like *that* Apollo. This one is their disgusting son."

"Son—not *sun*…sorry, I mean Mr. and Mrs. Rivers have a son who is called Apollo?"

"Yes."

"And he's unkind to you?"

"Yes."

"Perhaps they've made him that way… Are they all unkind?"

"Oh, yes."

"How?"

"They hit me and shout. They throw things at me. They took the sugar off the tea tray to make it look like my fault. They say I can't possibly remember my parents—but I can, I can!"

To her horror Hope found two tears had burst from her eyes. She shook them angrily away and said, "All these people say I'm a dolt with my head in the clouds. That all I can do is be a maid-of-all-work, and do as I'm told and be grateful, but—but—"

"You don't believe it?"

"Yes—no—I don't know—"

"What do you *want* to be, Hope?"

Hope stared at Cassandra, and Cassandra stared just as hard at *her,* almost as hard as she had stared on the step.

Very slowly Hope said, "When I'm alone sometimes, at my aunt's, even here, I act out the stories my parents told me. I play all the parts, or I play one part and imagine other people play the rest. Or I tell myself stories aloud, but I give them different endings, sometimes, or add things. But when my aunt caught me she shouted at me. She said, 'You can't live in Cloud-Cuckoo-Land,' and she sent me here. And here there isn't a moment to do anything much but work."

"Will you tell me one of the stories?"

Hope hesitated. Outside the sitting room, she could now hear running footsteps, cries, tremendous sneezes, and then a wild voice that sounded like Cassandra's husband: "No, don't fetch my wife—a-choo!—she'll be so upset—she'll have a turn, I expect, scream and so on—" and then a *bang*.

And Mrs. Rivers herself hysterically screaming, "Oh! He's going to faint—get the brandy!"

And Zeus the dog barking all through this.

And next Mrs. Rivers howling: "*Not* on the butterfly cases—catch him, someone!"

And then another incredible *crash*.

Hope and Cassandra both jumped up, suddenly giggling. When they stopped, a silence had fallen, and Hope told Cassandra the story called "Pandora's Box," not knowing that Cassandra already knew it. Cassandra didn't seem to mind.

When Hope finished, Cassandra leaned down and hugged her quite hard. And only then, sounding miles off, came yet one more crash, but smaller.

"Hope, do you want to be an actress?" asked Cassandra. "Do you want to act out stories and myths about wonderful things, and by acting make magic for other people, so they can be happy while *you're* being happy?"

"Do I? Is that it?"

Right outside the door Zeus barked in a different way, as if he were bark-saying, *Look out!*

"Hope, take this card."

Hope found Cassandra had pressed a visiting

card into her hand. Oddly, it seemed to have neither a name nor an address on it.

Cassandra said, "This isn't a question, Hope.
Now *I'm* going to tell you something. Try to
believe me. Try as hard as you can. Here we go.
Don't ever want anything bad for anyone. Want
the best for them, but also want the best for you,
too. Want your heart's desire. *Believe* in me, and
believe in yourself, and most of all believe in your
dreams!"

"But—" said Hope.

The door flew open. Mrs. Rivers rushed
through, with dust, moths, and bits of glass in
her hair.

"Oh!" she wailed. "Oh! Oh! That man has broken four glass cases. He *fell* on the last two."

"Dear me," said Cassandra. "*My* husband, do
you mean, or yours?"

"And your dog," screeched Mrs. Rivers, "has
broken a cut-glass decanter and drunk the best
brandy!"

Zeus hiccuped from the doorway.

Cassandra looked very serious. "How terrible. I'm afraid it can't have been good for him."

"*Oh!*"

"And I do apologize, of course."

Edmund, Cassandra's husband, now appeared,
reeling through the doorway. Mrs. Rivers ran

away across the room, but Mr. Rivers stormed in after him.

"How dare you, sir?"

"Ah, my head," moaned Edmund, still reeling carefully and stumbling into the table of tea and cakes, which flew everywhere.

"You have trodden in a bath-bun—you are *insane!*" roared Mr. Rivers.

"I suppose then you won't be interested in assisting my expedition to the tropics?" Edmund asked.

"The sooner you are there the better, but no! Get out of my house! Never darken my door again."

Edmund straightened up. He said calmly, "You have, in your unlikely garden, a *Quercus orichalcus.* I'm positive you didn't know. It's the Brazen or Golden Oak of the ancient world. But you, sir, don't deserve it." He then offered his arm to Cassandra, and they walked with perfect dignity from Number 15, Cavalry Square, followed by their hiccuping dog.

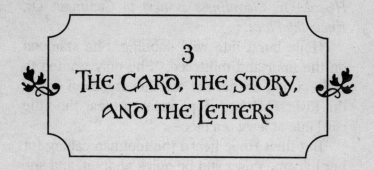

3
THE CARD, THE STORY, AND THE LETTERS

Normally Hope wouldn't have dared do what she then did. But today she ran away up the back stairs to the attic. Not till she got there did she look at the card Cassandra had given her.

And then Hope felt a leaden disappointment. For all that was written on the card, in gilded script, was this:

BELIEVE
AND
SEE—
STORIES
EQUAL
TRUTH.

Sometimes, at her aunt's house, grim old ladies had given Hope just such cards, which said things like, *Children should be Seen and not Heard*. Or, *Cleanliness is next to Godliness*. Or, *Know thy Place*.

Hope burst into wild sobbing. She stamped on the floor and muttered, "She only wanted to make a fool of me, the way her husband did of the Riverses!" And Hope meant to tear the little card into at least ten pieces.

But then Hope heard the footman calling for her to come down and be quick about it, and she rubbed away her tears and ran downstairs. This was the *real* world, and the *real* world was all there was. She'd better get used to it.

Two or three foul hours followed. The Riverses were in a very bad mood and soon got the servants in a worse one. Half of every meal was sent back to the kitchen with some complaint. Mrs. Crackle threw many things, including a salad, six roasted woodcocks, a small tureen of soup, and a trifle.

Late that evening, Apollo arrived home.

Hope, who had been dreading this event, now felt too dreary and depressed to care. So when she passed him in the hall, as she was carrying up some coal for the drawing-room fire, she took no notice of him. Apollo was thin, and tall for his age, and he peered at Hope with his black eyes. Then to her astonishment and sudden fear, he dragged off her cap and pulled her hair!

"Good evening, Miss Soppy. How are you? More soppy than ever? Pleased to hear it."

But Hope didn't reply. She just snatched back her cap and hurried past, nearly falling over Apollo's bags, which the footman had just carried in.

Then the door to Mr. Rivers's study opened. Apollo's father loomed out. "Don't dawdle, boy. In here at once."

Apollo bolted into the study. He had learned early on not to keep his father waiting.

The door was shut.

Mr. Rivers positioned himself before the fireplace, where the evening fire had been lit. He filled his pipe with tobacco and struck a match, and all the time Apollo stood as straight as he was able. He had been told from about six years old that he must always stand straight, keep his chin up, hide his feelings, and "be a man."

"Now, Apollo," said Mr. Rivers, puffing out smoke like a fat steam train, "I have a letter here from your headmaster, Mr. Ruff."

"Yes, sir?"

"He says he is quite displeased."

Apollo's heart sank—but not his head.

"I'm sorry, Father."

"He tells me you prefer horse-riding and birds-nesting to your books. Now, I'm glad you enjoy these manly pursuits. And I thank you for the two rare eggs you sent me last week. Luckily they weren't broken today. But if you are to become a great man, as you well know I wish you to, then you must pay more attention to your lessons."

Mr. Rivers withdrew the headmaster's letter from his waistcoat pocket and looked it over.

Apollo felt himself go hot and red, but kept his head up. Just as he had after the three times Mr. Ruff had personally caned him.

"'Mind wanders...'" read Mr. Rivers, "'daydreams...' Apollo! To daydream is unforgivable."

"It was only—"

"*Silence!*"

"I'm sorry, sir."

All at once Mr. Rivers gave a yelp, as if he had been stung by a bee. From the letter he shook a piece of glass and a small dead butterfly. "Do you see this?"

"Er—yes—"

"Confounded man, came in here, broke my glass cases. Hundreds of pounds of damage. And his appalling dog—no breed at all, some mongrel, and a *Greek* mongrel at that, I gather—it drank my brandy."

Apollo, as he often did when surprised, gaped like a fish.

"Glass everywhere," went on Mr. Rivers irritatedly. "I would have had the thing shot."

Presumably, thought Apollo, he meant the dog?

"But, Papa, you always say a dog's only as good as his master trains him to be—"

"Exactly. But I'd expect you to be soft on a dog. I recall how you blubbed and sniveled, Apollo, when your puppy died. Seven years old and sobbing like a girl."

Apollo's face turned white. He hung his head after all.

"Thank heavens I took a firm hand with you and taught you to stop all that. What a big baby."

More debris trickled from the letter. Angrily Mr. Rivers threw it down. "Where's all this mess coming from? Yes, boy, you can get out now. But remember what I said. Go and tell them you need some supper. Nothing rich, this late. Bread and butter."

"Thank you, sir."

As Apollo left the study, he met Hope again. She was carrying more coals, this time for Mrs. Rivers's sitting room.

"Don't you stare at me, Ugly! You've got a nerve." And he gave a vicious kick at the coal pail. Hope lost hold of it, and it fell with a rattle and bang. Black coal and coal dust streaked the walls and carpet.

"Now look what you've done, you clumsy, nasty girl."

"You did it, not me," Hope flared.

"Oh, answer back, will you? I'll tell Mother."

"Go and tell her, then!"

Hope stood there, face flaming, until Apollo had stalked away. Then in a panic she began to pick up the coals and tidy the rug, trying not to cry. But to her surprise, no one came to shout at her. (Apollo must have thought it beneath him to tell on her.) And when she finally took the coals in to Mrs. Rivers, the lady paid her no attention.

That night Hope didn't get up to bed until nearly eleven o'clock. When she entered her part of the attic, she saw Cassandra's card still lying there on the wooden stool.

Hope picked up the card. She read softly aloud, "Believe And See—Stories Equal Truth." It struck Hope then, for the first time, that even if these words weren't helpful and made no sense, neither were they unkind or bullying. In fact, they seemed almost to promise something nice. But what?

So she didn't tear up the card. She put it under her pillow. Hope was by now too tired to sleep at once. None of the other servants slept in her corner of the attic, although they sometimes came over to look out the window. By night Hope was utterly alone. So she began, in a low, soft voice, to tell herself the story she had told Cassandra, the story of Pandora's Box.

There were two brothers who were Titans. The Titans belonged to a giant race from the beginning of Time. Prometheus, the elder brother, gave mankind the gift of Fire, which he stole for them from the gods. This fire was magical. Not only did it give men power over cold and darkness, but it also gave them inspiration to think great thoughts and to create beautiful and cunning things. Until then, only the gods had had these powers. When they discovered what Prometheus had done, they were very angry.

Zeus, the god of thunder, decided to punish Prometheus, his brother Epimetheus, and mankind as a whole.

First, Prometheus was seized and chained to a distant crag (from which he only escaped long after). Then the gods made a woman out of clay, into which they blew the breath of life. On this creature they lavished every appealing quality. They called her Pandora—which meant all-gifted, or all-giving, depending on how you took it. But though beautiful, Pandora was selfish; though witty, she could be spiteful; and though intelligent, she was always in the grip of a burning curiosity and nosiness.

Epimetheus had meant to be wary of Zeus, but when he saw the amazing Pandora, he forgot.

So as not to alarm his beloved, the giant reduced himself and became mortal height. He and Pandora were married, and seemed as happy as any ordinary couple who have fallen in love.

Before his imprisonment, Prometheus had given into his brother's charge a large box on a scale with their own normally gigantic height. Prometheus had told Epimetheus he must guard this Box, and that it must never, *ever,* be opened.

(At this point in the story, Hope's mother had explained to Hope that some people said the Box might have been a Jar. "But they kept their clothes in chests, so it might have been a chest, or box, after all.")

Jar or Box, Pandora obviously soon noticed it. "What's in *there?*" she asked Epimetheus.

Epimetheus said he didn't know, and added that the Box must never be opened. "A tiny peek?" cooed nosy Pandora. Epimetheus asked her to please forget the Box.

This, of course, was hard to do. It took up a lot of room, even in the colossal house of the Titan, where Pandora and the shrunk-down Epimetheus wandered about like two little mice.

As well as clever, Pandora was sly. She simply waited until Epimetheus was out. Then she found a long ladder, propped it on the side of the Box, and climbed up. At the top she picked the lock. How she lifted the lid is another matter. Possibly she had some help from *inside.*

As the lid swung back, out of the Box flew all

the Horrors of the world, which Prometheus had locked away there. Sadness and Badness, Sickness and Pain, Cruelty, Madness, Doom and Gloom, and many other, worse, things. Pandora howled as they flew away into the world to bring misery to mankind.

However, there was one other thing in the dreadful Box, which presently came fluttering out on rainbow wings.

"I stayed in the Box because I knew this hour would come," said the bright-winged maiden hovering there. "Now I shall go out into the world, to help men bear the trouble and sorrows which escaped, and also to help them see beyond them."

"Who are you?" asked Pandora (still curious).

"My name," said the winged maiden, "is Hope."

In the dark attic of Number 15, Cavalry Square, Hope said softly, "And my mother said she called me Hope after the rainbow creature from the Box. And that was why she knitted me the rainbow gloves, too."

The next moment, Hope was fast asleep.

And what *seemed* the next moment after that, the other maid was shaking her roughly because it was time to get up again.

To make everything worse, at ten in the morning there was another scene in the kitchen, because Mrs. Rivers had complained about the state of the front step. It still had paw marks all over it.

"Get out and do it over, you lazy bundle!" shouted Mrs. Crackle, weighing the most throwable teapot menacingly.

And the footman added, as he had yesterday, "You should be grateful, Glover. You get the easy jobs," he lied.

But no sooner was Hope back at the front door than she saw a horse-drawn cab pull into Cavalry Square. This drew up outside Number 15, and out stepped a slender, tall lady, who, for a second, Hope took for Cassandra.

However, this lady was older, and she was more plainly, yet also more elegantly, dressed. And while her hair, too, was gold, it was a paler, smokier gold. In one hand she held a large brown-paper parcel and in the other, a white envelope.

She walked right up to Hope and at once held out the envelope.

"For Mrs. Rivers?" Hope asked.

"You're Hope, aren't you?" said the lady gently.

"Yes, madam."

"Then it's for you. I'm Miranda, Cassandra's sister."

It was as if the sun broke out in Hope's mind. She couldn't help smiling and smiling up at the elegant lady called Miranda.

"But now," said Miranda, "I'd better go and speak to Mrs. Rivers."

A cloud covered the sun. Hope's face fell. "I don't think she'll like that—"

"No, I'm sure she won't. But there we are."

And Miranda swept through the door and into the hall, imperious as a queen.

Hope held the white envelope a moment more, then slipped it into her apron pocket. It felt heavy and full of something *good.* On one corner, Hope had glimpsed the drawing of a strange animal with a long mane and a single spiral horn. Hope recognized it from the stories she knew. The lady had drawn a *unicorn* on her letter.

"My stars!"

Hope looked back into the hallway.

"Well, I never!"

"The sauce!"

Several of the servants were pressed up against the door of Mrs. Rivers's sitting room, listening. This included the butler, who had just shown Miranda into the room.

Hope got up quietly and managed to creep up and listen, too.

She heard Mrs. Rivers announce in her most fearsome voice, "If you are the sister of that young *woman,* we have nothing to say to each other."

Then Miranda spoke.

"I'm sorry, Mrs. Rivers, that you have never heard of the virtue of forgiveness."

("My," said the footman admiringly, "she sounds just like royalty.")

"Forgive? Virtue? All those cases of my husband's insects ruined. And that dreadful dog— called *Zeus,* I believe. Why, pray, call a dog *that?*"

"He's called Zeus," said Miranda reasonably, "for his thunderous bark."

"Madness! Oh—what's this?"

"Edmund has written you a check to cover the breakages."

There was a long silence.

Then Mrs. Rivers said, awkwardly, "Some of the specimens were irreplaceable…"

"Yes," said Miranda, "so many people have trapped them, they no longer exist."

"Oh, um, yes… This is very generous—the check, that is."

"Indeed," said Miranda. "It will put back the date of Edmund's expedition by some weeks. But please don't feel guilty, Mrs. Rivers. Lord Brassbone has now taken an interest in Edmund's work."

"Lord Brassbone!" exclaimed Mrs. Rivers. She was evidently much impressed.

"And, as a further token of our regret," said

Miranda, "please accept this small present for your son, Apollo."

There was another silence.

The servants were unprepared when the door suddenly flew open and Miranda came sweeping out. They all caught sight of a speechless Mrs. Rivers holding a large brown-paper parcel and a check. Hope, looking up, saw something even stranger. The queenly Miranda *winked* at her. Then she was gone.

A few minutes later, Hope was back kneeling by the front step, rubbing and scrubbing, and nothing might have happened at all, except for the heavy letter in her pocket.

Oddly though, the difficult step was soon clean, and next it sparkled. It was now the best front step in the whole of Cavalry Square. Perhaps all London!

Hope's reward for this success, however, was only lots more work to do. It wasn't until after the midday dinner that she was able to slip away and open her letter. To her surprise, the first thing that fell out was another, slightly smaller letter in an envelope. This envelope, too, had a unicorn head drawn on it. On it was written only one name: *Sebastian*.

Hope felt rather upset for a moment. She knew she mustn't read a letter addressed to someone else. Then she found the paper tucked in behind it, and this was covered with writing, and began, *Dear Hope...*

Dear Hope,
My sister, Miranda, has given you this letter, and I think you won't mind too much that she has read it. Because, you see, she and I shared an adventure seventeen years ago (when I was just a year younger than you are now). And you, I think, are about to have another adventure very like ours— but very different, and all your own.

Miranda and I, and our father, went to that place I told you of, the College of Magical Knowledge, but that place was in a wonderful land, a land of sea and islands and—magic. We traveled there on a beautiful ship. If you remember, the card I gave you had six words written on it. Believe And See—Stories Equal Truth. And if you read just the first letters of those six words, they spell the name BASSET. Which is the ship's name. On our voyage in the ship we found that all the creatures of myth and story really do exist. They live in this magical world we call the Lands of Legend, which somehow lies next to our world, or even inside our own world, and can sometimes be reached, if you believe hard enough and never let go of your dreams.

When we left there, Miranda and I had each received from the fairies (of course, they're real, too) a special gift. I was given an enchanted jewel on a pendant, and Miranda, an enchanted dress. When wearing that dress, I must tell you, Miranda tamed a unicorn! Yes, truly they do exist. But you have to believe in them before you can see them, and even then it isn't always possible. Unfortunately, our world, which so many people call the real world, can get in the way. It can make you think too much of the wrong and unimportant things. It can make you doubt everything, including yourself. But for you, Hope, I think it won't. And why do I think that? Because the moment I saw you, the pendant jewel, which I always keep with me, grew hot. And when I looked at it, it glowed. Later, when I spoke to Miranda, she showed me the dress, and it too was glowing with a wild warm light.

Something is going to happen to you, Hope! Something astonishing, exciting, perhaps even very startling, but something magical. Something good. And because I'm so sure that you'll soon be aboard the Basset, I've enclosed—I hope you won't mind—

*a letter to my first and oldest friend. He is a
little gray dwarf, and the sweetest of men—
and once he saved my life. I see him still in
my dreams, as Miranda does, just as we
both see the* Basset *then. Asleep, we still
visit the Lands of Legend. But it would
make me so happy to know that when you
meet Sebastian—how I envy you!—you'll
put this letter into his dear hand.*

    Be glad and lucky, Hope.

With all my fondest wishes,
Cassandra

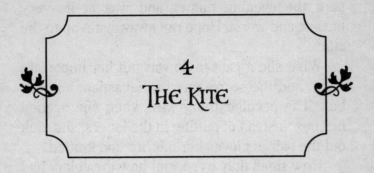

4
THE KITE

Most of the rest of that day passed in a sort of mist. Nothing was quite real—a thing that the so-called real world didn't seem to like. It kept trying to grab Hope's attention back to itself. She was given endless extra-tiring tasks. She tripped on the upstairs landing and fell down, to be shouted at by the butler. And belowstairs, Mrs. Crackle threw potatoes at her.

Despite all this, Hope felt as if she were floating several inches above the ground. One minute she believed everything in the letter. Then she didn't. And then she did again. But through it all she felt happy and excited, as she thought she must have when she was very little on the night before her birthday or Christmas.

In the end, at about five o'clock in the after-

noon, when the kitchen was getting ready to pre-
pare the evening dinner and was at its very
busiest and worst, Hope ran away again up to the
attic.

What she meant to do was put her important
letter, and the secret one for Sebastian, into her
box. The peculiar thing was, when she opened
her box, instead of putting in the letters, she took
out the pair of gloves her mother had knitted.

How small they were, and how the colors had
faded. Hope lifted them up against her face and
thought she could faintly smell the scent of jasmine, which her mother had worn.

Then there was a lot of shouting below.

In the attic was one tiny diamond-shaped window, which looked out on the Riverses' private
garden. None of the servants was supposed to
look out at the garden. Of course, they did, from
the attic and from everywhere else they could.

The garden was enclosed by high stone walls,
like all the other gardens in the square, except
the public one in the middle. It had neat lawns,
and flower beds with nothing much in them yet,
and some evergreen bushes cut into ball shapes
and cones. There was a white summerhouse, and
then a pond, and then a kitchen garden with rasp-
berry canes, asparagus beds, and a gooseberry
bush. Everything looked rather bare because the
spring leaves were only just coming. There was

one always-impressive thing in the garden, however. This was a huge tree with a great corded trunk, which was taller even than the house. It grew at the end of the lawn just before the summerhouse. In the summer, the leaves turned a brilliant golden green. Now it was filmed with a soft haze of buds.

Cassandra's husband, Edmund, had said something about a Golden Oak in the garden— was this the tree? Whether it was or not, there was a lot of fuss going on around it now. Two maids and the butler and the footman were there, and then there was Mrs. Rivers, too—and there was Apollo, dark and angry and embarrassed and sulky all at the same time.

Inevitably Apollo looked straight up at that moment, saw Hope, and pointed at her.

Everyone turned up their heads. Mrs. Rivers glared.

Hope, scared, darted away from the window. She stuffed the letters back in her pocket, and, not really thinking, pushed in the gloves as well.

Below, they were all shouting her name. Or she thought they were.

Quickly, she dashed downstairs, sure that now something really awful would happen.

But when she reached the garden by the back stairs, no one was there but the footman and Apollo.

"Go on, you," Apollo was saying. "Do as you're told."

"I can't, Master Apollo. I told you. I'm afraid to. I'll fall."

"What a great baby. Why don't you blub and cry?"

The footman went pink.

"I c-can't, Master Apollo. I get dizzy."

"Go up that tree, I tell you. I bet even this stupid *girl* could do that!" Apollo added, scowling at Hope.

"Why would I?" said Hope.

"Because I say so."

"Why don't *you* climb up?" demanded Hope.

Apollo frowned worse. "I would, wouldn't I? But Mama says I'll tear my shirt or something, and I'm not to. I climb up higher than that when I go birds-nesting, all right."

"That's *cruel*," said Hope.

"What do you know about it?"

"You take eggs away from mother birds and put them in a glass case, where they can't hatch, and the new birds don't get born."

"So what."

"So it's cruel and mean and *stupid!*"

The footman, although he was older than both of them, stood staring. Suddenly he turned around and ran back into the house.

"Rotten coward!" yelled Apollo.

"*You're* the coward," cried Hope, "being so horrible to a boy who can't answer back because he's your servant."

"You're a servant and *you* answer back. I'll get you dismissed!" roared Apollo. "Yes, that's what I'll do."

Hope went cold and her legs turned to water. She'd been right, the awful thing had happened. She would be sacked and have to go back and live with the ghastly purple aunt, and Hope would never hear the end of it. Indeed, the aunt might disown her, and then Hope would have to beg on the streets. (The aunt had threatened her with this fate once or twice.)

But she wouldn't beg now from *Apollo*. Oh, no.

The sun was going into the west. The light was changing, and things looked strange in it.

Hope straightened her shoulders and looked Apollo in the eye. She said, "All right. I'll go up the tree. Why do you want me to?"

Apollo's mouth dropped open again. He closed it with a snap. "It's the kite. Stupid kite. I just let it go up, to see, and the wind got it and dragged it straight across into the oak tree. It's caught fast. It'll get torn. Who cares?" He turned his back on Hope and gazed down the garden. "Mother was in a flap. It was a present from that tall blond woman, or her sister, or something."

"Miranda—Cassandra—"

"Daft names. Yes, them. Anyway, it cost a lot, Mother said. So it matters."

Hope didn't quite know anymore what she felt or thought, if she was afraid or angry or what. But she found herself going over to the tree trunk, which in the strange light looked almost like metal.

Apollo glanced at her. "Yes, Crackle said *you* ought to go up for the kite. Always got your head in the clouds. So up a tall tree's the best place for you."

Had Hope ever before climbed a tree? She didn't know. But oddly, she seemed able to climb this one. She thought she'd heard someone once say, "Don't look down, look up." So she did. First she caught a low bough with her hands, then she swung up onto it. Then she caught another bough, and, using the thicker branches like a kind of ladder, she was soon quite high.

Hope was strong from all the hard work. She found that the climb wasn't difficult at all. And the tree had a lovely smell, and she saw now all the ripe fat shiny buds, each with just a little green frill where the leaf was beginning.

She wondered what Apollo was doing, but as she mustn't look down, she didn't see. She couldn't see the kite, either. But Miranda had brought it. If Miranda and Cassandra had brought the kite, the kite would be magical and special.

But then, why bring that beast Apollo anything?

Apollo, too, had been puzzled earlier in the day, when his father and mother called him into the drawing room and showed the kite to him.

It was as tall as he was, and looked as if it were made of silk. It was colored blazing orange, and on it was an outline, in dark blue and gold, of a ship with full rigging.

"You must write a letter to thank them at once," said Mrs. Rivers.

Mr. Rivers added, "But don't thank them too much. Their behavior was disgraceful."

Apollo then had to sit down in his father's study and write an awkward thank-you note which mustn't say thank you too much. It took over an hour.

The day was very boring, full of tutors and visits. The adult talk was about business, and Apollo knew he should listen, because when he grew up he would be an important man in business or politics.

But somehow his mind kept going back to the kite.

Finally, after tea, he had been able to escape to the garden. There was only a light breeze, and the garden wasn't the best place to try the kite, yet something made him want to. So he let out the kite on its golden string.

For a second it soared up, like a flame on the late blue of the sky. And Apollo seemed to feel his heart leap up with it. It looked so free, the kite, so full of possibility.

And then the next second it turned over and rolled into the top of the oak tree.

He knew at once to tug it would be to tear it. Apollo felt bad. It was as if he felt sorry for the kite. But then he only felt sorry for himself. He knew his father and mother would be furious. Despite what he had boasted, he wasn't sure, either, he could climb that high himself.

To start with, Apollo tried to get the butler's help. Then the footman and maids came out. Then Mrs. Crackle came to see because she was nosy, but she soon lost interest again and went. In the end Mrs. Rivers appeared. Her face was like a hard, bad-tempered white plate.

"I'll climb up," said Apollo, uncertainly.

"Of course you won't. You'll get filthy and ruin your clothes. No. The kite must stay there until the gardener has time to get it tomorrow. How annoying of that woman to give you such a thing and cause such trouble. You are a thoughtless, wicked boy."

Then Apollo wanted to get the kite very badly. It might rain in the night. The wind might rise and hurl the kite away.

Just then Apollo saw—not Hope upstairs at the attic window, but the tail of the kite somehow blowing about in the upper branches. He pointed at it, and for some reason everybody shouted.

They didn't shout, as Hope had thought, her name. They hadn't seen her. It was only "Look at that now," and "Some bird's got hold of it," and "No, it's the wind." Then everyone remembered other things they had to do and went indoors. And Apollo, left with the footman, said, "If you climb the tree I'll give you sixpence." But the footman said, "I can't stand heights, Master Apollo."

Now, watching Hope climbing straight up the great tree, easy as a cat, Apollo went sick with shame. She was a *girl*. She was a *servant*. It wasn't even her kite, and he hadn't offered her any money. He'd said he'd get her sacked, but Apollo had forgotten that; he hadn't meant it.

"What a little pest she is," growled Apollo.

The sun sank behind the summerhouse right then, and a deep smooth shadow seemed to cover everything in the garden, all but the shining top of the oak.

Apollo ground his teeth. He must "be a man." He took off his jacket, folded it, and put it aside.

He could no longer see Hope. She had vanished like the kite in the branches high above. Apollo had the feeling the tree was suddenly many miles high. He might have to climb for days and nights to reach the top. But if Hope could do it, so could he.

He sprang for the first bough.

As Apollo started at the bottom, Hope had reached the top of the oak tree, but for a moment she didn't know it.

The boughs and branches had seemed to go on and on. Then suddenly she was reaching for the next bough—but it wasn't there. For a second she felt giddy. But then she realized that she was—or seemed to be—on top of the world!

What a sight she saw then.

It was the perfect time of day, because the sun was just setting. The sky was like a sheet of gold that melted into blue at one end, and into rose at the other. At the rose end, the sun was balanced like a ball on the city of London. The smoke of all the spring chimneys had draped the sun, so you could look right at it, and against it a thousand differently shaped buildings stood up black.

The city looked quite enormous, and endless. Streets and houses, roofs and squares, church spires and parks. Hope could see tiny people, too, going along, and tiny carriages pulled by horses the size of sparrows, and farther off, the size of beetles. But right across everything ran a gleaming spill of gold, like a ribbon fallen from the sky. At first Hope didn't know what it was—and then she did. It was the River Thames. And beyond it was the other thing she knew of but had never before seen—the great dome of St. Paul's Cathedral.

Hope sat on the bough, looking and looking. She had forgotten Apollo, even forgotten the kite.

Birds flew over, making patterns, their wings gilded. The western sky, where the sun was now sinking, turned crimson.

"I wish I could stay up here forever—"

Something rustled, and Hope glanced down at the tree. Perhaps a bird was there (in fact it was Apollo scrambling below), but what she saw was the kite. It was curious she hadn't spotted it before.

Hope gazed at it. It was a nice kite, but Apollo had said it was worth a lot of money and that was nonsense. It was a very ordinary kite, of paper, with a sort of squiggle on it that might have been meant to be a picture, though she couldn't make out of what. If she leaned over and carefully pulled it loose, she might be able to drop it down to the lawn.

When she thought that, Hope looked right down at the lawn.

"Oh! The ground's miles away!" she cried in

terror. It did seem to be. The house was only a small pile of roofs below, and the garden looked as small as a handkerchief.

Hope clung to the bough in fright. And just then the last of the sun winked out, and the sky, strangely, seemed to become much *brighter.*

And in this bright light Hope saw the kite was made not of paper, but of silk. And on it was the picture of a ship, very delicately and finely drawn, with three rigged masts. Under the picture ran two words in another language (actually Latin): CREDENDO VIDES. Hope didn't understand what this meant, but somehow just the look of the words made her suddenly feel brave, reckless, and excited, although she didn't know why.

So she gazed out again at the sunset sky— and saw something truly astonishing.

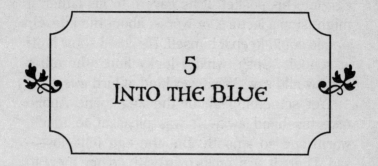

5
INTO THE BLUE

When Apollo was, he thought, nearly all the way up the tree, he paused. He felt rather shaky, and this annoyed him.

Then he noticed, only a foot in front of him among the boughs, a big untidy bird's nest made of twigs and grass.

"Well, what's this?" said Apollo, in his "manly" voice.

It seemed to him he had never seen a nest like it, even in a bird book with illustrations. And when he craned forward and peered in, there lying in the nest was a single, very large egg. It was the palest blue in color. And when he reached out to it, it felt slightly warm. It was almost bigger than his hand.

"I've never seen one like that," said Apollo. The parent bird must have flown off, startled by the sound of climbing. It would be easy to slip the egg into his pocket. If he gave it to his father, it might stop a lecture, or worse, about the kite. Or Apollo could keep it himself. He could show it off at school. "Gosh, what a lucky find," the other boys would say. "Whatever kind of bird *was* it?"

Yet something about the egg made Apollo take his hand away. It was pleasant to touch, warm and so smooth. But the egg felt—lost—sad. There it was, on its own, with no one there to protect it. Only a thief. But that was silly. It was just an old egg. What did it matter?

Then the craziest sort of noise began in the tree and all around. Apollo clung to the branches in alarm. It sounded as if not one or two birds, but fifty or a hundred birds were flying back, and very fast.

Hope, some way higher up and looking over London, already knew what was happening.

At first she had thought the colored wisps flying up through the sky were clouds. Then she thought perhaps they were pieces of washing blown off lines—they came in ones and twos, and then in dozens.

But they had marvelous colors, mauve and red and tangerine and silver—some sparkled, some flashed in the sunset like mirrors, and all had fluttering tails—

They were *kites*.

They were coming from everywhere, all over the city. As she stared, she saw new ones unwind from the tops of church spires, or sail up out of parks. They blew over the faces of tall stern statues, and unrolled up chimneys with the evening smoke. They played with weather vanes, now spinning one way and now another, before darting out into the sky. Kites—were there really so many kites in London? And all of them, great and small, dancing or dawdling, were flying this way, toward the Golden Oak in the garden in Cavalry Square.

Hope had forgotten almost everything by now. Certainly she'd forgotten to be afraid. She simply sat on the top bough, all eyes. And as she did this, Apollo's kite of orange silk, all by itself, floated up from the branches, no longer caught, and hung in the air beside her.

Then all the other kites, which by now crowded the sky over London, began to hurry. They came skipping and whipping in. As soon as the first ones reached the great kite, they flew up around it. Then more arrived and did the same. Once they touched it, all the kites seemed to grow together with the big kite. And so in moments, this kite was twice its size, and then six times its size, and then twenty times—and then it seemed to fill the sky, and it was no longer a kite, or a flock of kites. It was a patchwork quilt of glorious colors and spangles.

This beautiful thing then glided down until it was level with Hope's feet. There it stopped quite still. It was as if it said to her, *Come on. You know what I am, now.*

Perhaps it wasn't the sensible thing to do. But as Miranda or Cassandra would have told her, "You seldom find magic by being sensible." Hope of course knew, you must *never* step off a tree, unless a magic carpet is there and clearly visible. One was.

She took a deep breath, and walked off the tree onto the carpet of kites.

For a moment, the carpet was quite still—or almost. It rocked just a little, gently, like a boat on a calm river.

Overhead, the sky was turning into a shining twilight blue, and stars were appearing.

Then the kite carpet gave a huge lunge. There was a sort of shouting or screaming noise, and the sound of branches breaking. A ripple ran over the carpet, which rolled Hope forward and into a dip at its middle. Hope only sat up again and laughed. They were moving. She patted her pocket where the letters and her gloves were. Then she tore off her maid's cap and threw it over the carpet's side with a cry of gladness.

The rumbling and rolling steadied as the carpet picked up speed. Hope had no way of knowing that the upheaval had been caused by what was caught up on the underside.

Apollo had grasped the tree firmly as the returning birds began to attack him. And he hadn't called out, partly because he didn't have time.

But then he saw that what slapped at him was not birds at all, but the long tails of several hundred kites. They were decorated with bows and streamers and were all sorts of colors, but their slaps stung him, and they got snagged on his buttons and in his hair. Soon he was all tangled up in them. And then to his horror, they were pulling him up through the tree in a shower of twigs.

Apollo fought, and he yelled, but somehow the tails of three kites went into his mouth and he could only splutter.

Suddenly he was lifted right out of the tree. He went cold with fear.

All London lay below, the Rivers house like a dollhouse, and above was an enormous dark blue sky with stars all over it like dropped sixpences.

The kites had him fast. He could hardly move. He hung below them and saw their huge carpet stretched over him like a shadow.

Apollo finally couldn't make a sound, he was so scared. He couldn't even think. So he trailed there, pulled through the air under the flying carpet (his mouth wide open, even with the kite tails still in it, because he, too, knew what a flying carpet was), carried away just as Hope was, into the sky.

The carpet flew all night.

Although Apollo had a horrible journey, and may have cried a bit, or perhaps his eyes were irritated by the wind, and in the end he fell asleep, worn out from the buffeting of that same wind, Hope had a lovely time.

She sat in the dip and saw the land sail by below, and the night and the stars and the moon sailing with her. She, too, slept at last, but it was a wonderful sleep.

She woke when the sun had been up for some time, and then, when she looked, she saw over the carpet's side a glittering blueness everywhere below.

"It's the sea," said Hope.

She thought she had passed over seas in the night, too. She had noticed, she thought, ships far down on the dark water, and once a tall tower that shed a beam onto the waves—a lighthouse. But this sea was not the same. It was hard to say why not. It looked so clean and the blue was so brilliant.

Hope wasn't hungry or thirsty. The smell of the fresh air, the adventure, were enough.

She crawled along the carpet to its forward edge, and looked—fearlessly—down.

Dotted over the sea were chains of islands.

They caught the sun and white mountains gleamed, and there were dark woods or long slopes of grass, and here and there might be glimpsed buildings that were gone before Hope could properly make them out.

The carpet definitely flew lower now. Hope could see the ripples that creamed about the islands, and sometimes animals galloped over the open grass. And once, on a rock out in the sea, she noted the glimmer of two shining things—one of which looked like long blue hair, and the other like a long blue fish tail—

"Was it a *mermaid?*"

A few minutes after this, the carpet flew around the curve of a large mountainous island that on the near side was covered by thick woods and forest.

On the open sea beyond there lay at anchor a small, exquisite ship. It was like a piece of jewelry, and in the sunlight it shone like gold, and the sails like pearls. A banner curled out on the sky, the color of turquoise.

"The *Basset?*" said Hope. "It is? It *is*."

And she was leaning over, trying to read the name of the ship—since the carpet now seemed to be dropping lower and lower—when a strange shadow fell across the sea below.

It was not the shadow of the carpet. It was far, far larger.

"But it's almost," said Hope aloud, "in the shape of a great bird—"

And she turned to look up at the sky.

An enormous cloud hung there above her, and it was indeed shaped like a bird, the long neck outstretched and wings spread wide—and through the middle of it writhed white knots of lightning.

The sky had been quite clear, but now it began to alter. The blue went greenish and dark. A gust of wind rushed over, and to her horror Hope saw the great wings of the cloud bird *flap*. Then there was a clap of thunder, close, deafening, and awful.

And then something even more terrible happened.

Even without the storm bird, it was what most people would have expected to happen. Apollo had certainly expected it every minute. So *he* wasn't surprised, though he howled.

Hope shrieked. No wonder.

All the kites abruptly separated from each other. As they did so, large rifts of dark air appeared, and straight through one of these fell Hope—Apollo was already tumbling.

Neither saw the other. Both were too terrified. And the sky, flailed by the storm, seemed to tumble with them in chunks.

Overhead, through the now boiling and

shapeless clouds, the kites were flitting off in every direction. They gleamed and glinted as they did so, and vanished one by one like heartless bubbles.

Apollo hit the sea with a splash. The waves had turned coal blue and surging. He didn't see that he was quite near the forested island.

Twenty seconds later, and half a mile away, Hope, too, plunged into the angry water. She fell down and down.

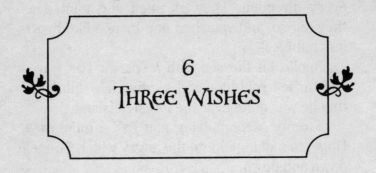

6
THREE WISHES

As she sank, Hope saw the lashing blue of the sea calm and change to emerald. Fish dashed by. But this didn't help.

She didn't know how to swim. She'd managed not to open her mouth, but her nose and ears and eyes were full of water. Soon she would need to take a deep breath—and there would be nothing but water to breathe.

All the while she kept feeling something bobbing against her hand. At last she looked at it, and even in her panic Hope could see at once what it was. A lamp—not the ordinary sort you might find in a house, but more like a kind of squashed-down teapot, with a handle at one end and a spout at the other. It was made of a dull metal that looked as if it needed a good rub.

Hope thought confusedly, *It's like a magic*

lamp in the Arabian Nights. *And* if *you rub it, the magic sprite inside has to come out—*

None of this, of course, seemed important. All that was important was not falling deeper and deeper into the sea and farther and farther away from the air she needed to breathe.

But the lamp kept bobbing against her. And now Hope found she'd taken hold of it. For a moment she didn't know why. Then she did. She rubbed the lamp as hard as she could.

There was a great *whooosh*. Something like thick smoke puffed from the spout of the lamp and coiled upward in the water. It wasn't smoke, but a wriggling smoky curious creature with a turban and big yellow eyes. Hope remembered what it was called. A *genie*.

"O Mistress of the Lamp, your wish is my command!" cried the genie in a high-pitched, squeaky voice.

Hope, though, couldn't speak in the sea. She pointed frantically to her mouth.

The genie gave a smoky smile that showed lots of fanged teeth, and waved one arm. From out of nowhere an enormous slice of cake came rushing at Hope. It hit her quite hard on the lips.

Hope, bursting for air, now had to shake her head wildly, fight off the cake (which kept trying to get into her mouth), and scowl an unspoken *No*.

The genie looked disappointed. It didn't seem to know where they were, and that therefore Hope was going to want only one thing. "I thought you were hungry, O Mistress of the Lamp. Thirsty, then?"

Hope found she had to dodge in quick succession a glass of lemonade, a cup of tea, and a mug of hot milk. She was desperate. There was nothing else for it. She opened her mouth and choked with her last inch of air: "Drowning! Help!" There was no proper sound, only bubbles, but:

"Ah!" said the genie.

There came a kind of thud. The water swirled and everything turned over, and Hope, spluttering, was flung up from the sea in a gush of water and small furious fish.

The fish dropped back into the sea. Hope hung dripping in the air.

For a while all she could do was cough and gasp. When she could, she stared around her. The storm had ended as swiftly as it had come, and the sea was almost still, save for a tiny whirlpool that marked where she and the genie had come up. And as for the genie—it was very like pictures she had seen of genii in books. It was manlike in a way, but also animal-like, like a cat perhaps. It was holding her in one coil of its smoky tail, which was almost *snake*like, the other

end of which *snaked* back into the lamp spout...
somehow Hope hadn't let go of the lamp. But
where—where had the *Basset* gone?

"Was that all right, O Mistress of the Lamp?"

"Yes, thank you," croaked Hope.

She thought the genie looked proud of itself.
It patted its turban and said, "Wasn't bad, was it?
After all this time. What would you like next, O
Mistress? And, er, perhaps you wouldn't mind
saying, 'I wish' this time. It helps my concentra-
tion."

"You mean—are there two more wishes?"

"Of course. Once I am out of the lamp, three
wishes each time. The food and drink were my
misunderstanding and don't count."

"Then—I wish I was dry."

"Quick as a flash!" squawked the genie. It
waved both its arms and Hope, who had felt drier
already from the warming sun, was drenched by
an icy shower that fell suddenly from nowhere.

"Oops. Oh dear. So sorry. I'm a bit—er—" the
genie blinked, *"out of practice."*

"Yes," said Hope, wringing out her hair.

"Thousands of years," rambled the genie,
"just bobbing about in the sea. Thrown from Sinbad's ship, you know," it added regretfully. "Or
was it Sinbad's great-grandson's ship? Let me
see. Could it have been his great-grandson's
nephew's aunt's ship?"

Talk of ships made Hope quickly look around again, and now, to her great relief, she did spot the *Basset,* sparkling there across the water. *Reaching* the *Basset* would be the only problem.

"Genie, do you see that ship over there?"

"No, where? Oh, there. Mmn. Sinbad? Probably not."

"Please," said Hope, "I'd like to be on that ship. That is, I *wish* to be on that ship. Only, are you sure you can—"

There was a loud bang.

Hope had once fallen down stairs, and this felt very like that. She toppled and turned, and things hit her, and she *bounced.* And then there she was—ouch. Perhaps it wasn't quite how she would have preferred to arrive.

She was hanging upside down from what must be a mast, and far below on the deck, five concerned faces gazed up at her. Two other faces were only inches away. These were round and smiling and had black stovepipe hats pulled down so far over their eyes, Hope doubted they could see. They belonged to two little men perched on the mast like owls. Next instant (perhaps to be polite), they spun around and turned upside down, too. Then they hung there with her, giggling.

"Oh dear, oh dear," wailed the genie. "O Mistress of the Lamp, do excuse me." And it

unhooked her from the mast and wafted her
down to the deck below. The giggly, hatted little
men came rattling along with her in its coils.

So it was that Hope first met the noble
dwarves who crewed HMS *Basset*. She landed at
their feet in a muddle of genie and giggly gremlins.

(And she knew they were gremlins the next
minute because someone stepped forward and
helped her up, muttering, "Those gremlins are
into everything today.")

Hope looked up, then *down*. The dwarf was
shorter than she was. He had the kindest face
she had ever seen. Of course, she hadn't seen
many kind faces. And yet she recognized his
kindness—his absolute *goodness*—at once. It was
as if she were meeting an old friend. And so she
knew who he was, but she still asked, hesitantly,
"Sebastian?"

"Indeed I am. And you are Miss Hope Glover."

Hope felt happy—and then she nearly
screamed. "Your letter! I brought it all this way—
and now it'll be soaked—"

His face was wrinkled, but it was like a piece
of beautifully pleated, pale brown velvet. His gray
mustache, even when she was so upset, made
her want to laugh, although his beard you could
only respect. His spectacles magnified his bright
eyes.

"It's all right. I think, if you take the letter out, you'll find it's not been harmed."

Hope wasn't so sure, but she fished in her apron pocket—and pulled out a *fish*. This smacked her face with an annoyed tail and dived over the ship's side back into the sea. The letter came next. It was as dry as when Miranda first gave it to her. (The genie's magic?) Even the name hadn't smudged. *Sebastian* it read clearly.

"You see?" said Sebastian, taking the letter. "Believe first, *then* see."

"I—didn't quite believe," said Hope humbly.

"I'm sure you'll soon learn how."

At this moment the genie poured back down into the lamp with such force that Hope dropped it. She dropped it on the toe of an important-looking dwarf with red hair.

"Oh—I'm sorry—"

"Think nothing of it, Miss Hope. My name is Malachi. I am the captain of this ship."

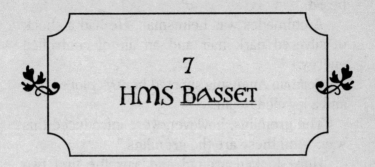

7
HMS BASSET

Captain Malachi introduced her to the three other dwarves.

Hope was impressed.

They were so elegantly dressed, in dapper suits and silk waistcoats, all embroidered, and Captain Malachi even had a strange violet-blue flower in his buttonhole. The dwarves were a combination of grave, serious, and gentle. Hope had met extremely grave people and *very* serious people, but they had always been unsmiling and bossy, certain they knew everything.

The dwarves *did* seem to know a lot, but they were comfortable with it. You felt you could take them as you found them, and that was how they would take you.

Sebastian was, Hope learned, the *Basset*'s first mate.

Eli was the bosun. He had a short, furry gray beard.

Archimedes was helmsman. He had a shock of silvered dark hair and an air of controlled energy.

Seaman Augustus sported honey-colored hair and a jeweled tiepin.

The gremlins, however, were introduced this way: "And these are the gremlins."

Hope looked around and saw the first two gremlins had been joined by what seemed to be about twenty more. But it was hard to be sure how many there really were. They all wore the same costume of red coat and tall black hat. They all had very big feet. And mostly they were darting about everywhere, some even pouncing up and down the rigging like top-hatted squirrels.

Hope couldn't help laughing. The gremlins seemed to approve of that.

One whipped off his hat and bowed to her. Another one jumped straight *into* the hat—which, although it didn't look it, was somehow big enough that he vanished instantly.

Then another gremlin took off *his* hat, shook it, and out fell the gremlin who had vanished—plus three oranges, a set of matching spoons, and a small table.

"But," said Hope, "however did all that fit in the hat?"

The gremlins were squeaking. Some were rolling over and over. They looked then rather like small, very odd children dressed up in top hats.

"Anything will go into a gremlin's hat, and usually does," remarked Archimedes. "It *may* come out later. Gremlins rarely think. They have inspirations—which are sometimes brilliant." However, he frowned.

"And sometimes," finished Augustus, "they're *not.*"

"You see, it's like the mind itself," said Sebastian. "Ideally it should have a careful, practical side. But also it needs its dreams, its laughter, its flashes of genius. Together, Method and a little Madness run the human machine. And that's, too, how we sail our ship."

"On the other hand," said Eli, "all those swans in the library were a bit *much!*"

No one explained this comment, so Hope gazed after those gremlins who were now swarming along a mast. The blue banner unfurled there, and she saw the gold lettering on it. Hope recognized the words; they had been on the kite: CREDENDO VIDES.

She turned to Sebastian. "What do those words mean?"

"By believing, one sees," Sebastian answered. There was a curious note of gentle pride in his voice as he said it.

Hope breathed out slowly. "Believing is seeing!"

With the gremlins—there were now more and more—bounding all around them (nearly tripping everyone up), the dwarves then showed Hope the way belowdecks.

Hope started to go down the little stair, then stopped. She was startled—but then she cried, "Somehow, it's exactly what I expected!"

For it was possible to see at once, and soon it was proved, that the *inside* of HMS *Basset* was quite unlike her upper parts. The ship was small—the deck quite tiny, and the masts, though brave, not mightily tall. But the inside of the ship was enormous, perhaps *endless*. Large rooms opened into larger rooms, and then into truly huge rooms. Corridors wound on and on, ladders and stairs ran up and down. There were rich furnishings and exotic objects everywhere—globes, maps, tapestries, weird ornaments, plants, stones, books—and also things that Hope couldn't identify at all. Hope didn't ask any questions, she had too many. She just stared and stared.

Then there was a door, and Sebastian said, here was her cabin.

"How did you know I was coming to your ship?" Hope asked shyly.

"I expect you'd know what a bird sounds like,

when it sings," said Sebastian, surprisingly.

"Yes."

"Well, we heard a sort of sound like birdsong, and so we knew the bird was there. Except that the song we heard was the sound of Hope Glover flying through like a bird, into the Lands of Legend, which is where we are now."

"Oh," said Hope. She smiled.

Once she was in her own cabin, she must have stayed exploring it for an hour or more. The bed was soft and hung with brocade curtains, like that of a lady. There was a lamp that, when lit, glowed like a pale sun. In a closet hung rows of dresses of the most incredible colors, and all trimmed with jewels and ropes of pearl, like garments from the best sort of fairy tale. When she was tiny she had loved dressing up, but there had been nothing like this, save in her imagination. Hope now chose a dress that glimmered like a dragonfly's wing. After she had put it on, she screwed up her maid's uniform and jumped up and down on it, seven or eight times.

Then she ran out, and Captain Malachi graciously escorted her to a late breakfast, or an early luncheon, in the dining saloon.

What a room!

They had to go down a lot of steps, and then Hope thought she had fallen back into the sea. She almost screamed that the ship had no bottom. But then she saw several gremlins turning somersaults on the invisible floor. Besides, there were chairs and a table and great ferns in urns, and even little tubbed trees, and flowers and marble statues—

The floor was made of some thick and magical glass. So were the walls. While the ceiling was painted deep blue with silver and gold stars.

On the glass on the *outside,* in the sea, glowing anemones and starfish had attached themselves to give the room a warm-cool, dreamy, green-blue, or sunny yellow-pink light.

And here they had lunch, even Archimedes, since the ship lay at anchor. (You could see the anchor chain curling down, outside the glass of the saloon floor.)

It wasn't like any meal Hope had ever had in her life. There was hot bread with melted cheese, hard-boiled eggs and lettuce, little potatoes lightly fried in olive oil and green herbs, a pudding full of grapes, fresh apricots, and pancakes with chocolate sauce.

After the breakfast-lunch, Hope had a pot of mint tea all to herself.

The dwarves talked to her, she thought, as if she were an adult. That is, they treated her with interest, courtesy, and kindness. They listened when she spoke, and replied. But in a way she didn't know what to say to them. It was all so delightful—yet unknown. And if she really started to ask questions, she felt she wouldn't stop.

At last, the lunch made Hope fall fast asleep, there at the table. And when she woke up, she was lying on a sofa in the magical dining room, and beyond the glass, about thirty feet away in the sea, she could make out two mermaids swimming by, with a porpoise on a leash.

But then the ship gave a sort of jump. The mermaids and porpoise fled away into the deeps of the water.

Hope hadn't been sure what to do about the lamp with the genie, so she'd left it in her cabin. Now she wondered if she should have kept hold of it.

But as she jumped up, Sebastian appeared.

"Don't be alarmed," he said, "the gremlins are being very busy. One just upended a grand piano out of his hat. I think it's their roundabout way of saying they think we should use the Wuntarlabe."

"What is a—voon-ter-lobb?"

"The Wuntarlabe shows us the way the ship must go. Come and see," said Sebastian.

So they went upstairs and into another room. All the dwarves had gathered there, and on a table stood a bizarre and magnificent object, gleaming with silver, copper, and other metals. It had dials and gears, and was formed in a graceful if unusual shape. Arrows pointed in all directions and gems winked and shimmered. It was pretty as a toy. Yet a sense of power streamed from it.

Archimedes was setting the gears, in a practised, accustomed way.

"And now," said Eli, "those gremlins."

Two gremlins bounded at once onto the table where the Wuntarlabe stood. One seemed to make a grab at it. The other bounced right over him and landed, nose down, in a dent in the silver and copper wheel.

The wheel instantly spun very fast. It went at such a speed, the second gremlin was catapulted off and landed in a curtain.

"Well!" exclaimed Eli, and his furry beard bristled.

The dials spun up and down, this way and that...some of them looked very like eyes which had suddenly gone crossed. Bells tinged, mechanisms twanged and clicked.

Then the largest arrow, which held a rich dark turquoise jewel, angled sharply right upward.

"Now look there. It's not working," muttered Augustus.

Archimedes grimaced. "Swans, pianos. The gremlins have made another mess of things."

The arrow pointed straight up at the ceiling,

there was no ignoring that.

Another bang shook the *Basset*.

"What now—"

The dwarves hurried on deck and Hope ran with them. It didn't seem to take as long as she might have expected, as if time and distance changed slightly, too, as well as size, as they came up from belowdecks. She marveled again at the small top deck, after the vast inner spaces. But at that moment, from a damson cloud directly above, there came a flare of lightning, and another loud bang—it was thunder.

Hope flinched. Had the strange storm bird returned? She couldn't see the shape of it this time in the cloud. Instead rain fell, bright as tinsel.

The dwarves didn't seem overly concerned, simply alert and ready. Reassured, Hope stayed with them on deck, watching the storm. Like the other, it lasted only a few minutes. The rain ended, the sun came out, and the cloud parted in the middle. Rays of gorgeous colored light poured through. In a moment a great luminous arch stood on the sea, seeming to rise and rise until it held the sky up on its back. It was a rainbow, but the best one Hope had ever seen.

"Isn't it lovely," she breathed. "It looks almost solid, like glass."

Captain Malachi spoke. "So the Wuntarlabe is

working after all. Our direction really is to be upward. We must ascend the rainbow."

"Can the *Basset* sail up a rainbow?" Hope asked Sebastian.

"Why not? Do you think we can?"

"Yes…" Hope added, "It'll be like sailing *up* a waterfall."

Seaman Augustus climbed a mast easily as a monkey to adjust the rigging; gremlins helped— in their own way…Eli, also helped or hindered by gremlins, raised the anchor, and Archimedes took his position at the helm.

A strong breeze blew from the rainbow. No, it didn't blow—it *pulled*. The *Basset*'s sails puffed forward in the strangest way, the ship's banner curled around into a circle. And they were off.

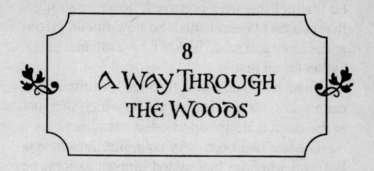

8
A Way Through
The Woods

Years ago, when he was only eight, Apollo had
been taught to ride and to swim. And during
summer holidays ever since, along with horse-
riding, he had swum every day. He was a strong
swimmer by now, and that was just as well.

When he fell into the sea, he had known to
hold his breath, lift his arms above his head as if
to dive, and wait for the force of the water to bob
him up to the surface. But it seemed to take a
long time. When he emerged, he trod water, getting his breath back. And as he did so, he looked
up into the clearing sky. Last rags of the sudden
storm and last wisps of red, purple, and amber
kites were scurrying away together.

Apollo knew something very peculiar had
happened. But he didn't believe in magic, just as
he didn't believe in ghosts, Father Christmas, or

even angels. Apollo's father had taught him early on that nothing ever occurred, however strange, that couldn't be explained. So now Apollo glared at the kites and said, "There'll be a rational explanation for all that."

Then he struck out, through the thankfully calm water, for the nearest shore, which was that of the mountainous and wooded island.

The sea had been very cold, but the sun was hot, and when he had pulled himself ashore, he lay down on the beach for a while. It was a good beach, with fine white sand. The storm might never have happened. The sea lapped with a musical noise. Above the beach, the woods began at once. They looked very thick and the trees very old and heavy with leaves. Far off, perhaps at the island's center, there showed something like two points of white drawn on the sky. They were the two peaks of the distant mountain.

Apollo would have liked to lie on the warm sand and sleep for half an hour. But people had always been telling him not to be lazy, to hurry up, to do this or that. So he made himself get up.

"I'd better explore these woods," he said. As he spoke, he had a definite feeling that exploring the woods wasn't really what he wanted to do at all.

But he wasn't a *coward*. Hadn't he climbed the huge oak tree? Hadn't he fallen out of the sky and swum across the sea?

There would be houses or a village in the woods, even a town on the far side of them. The people would be impressed by Apollo. They would help him.

"I suppose they'll speak English?" he asked. Of course, some incredible countries didn't, and he didn't, somehow, think he was in England anymore. Well, he would have to *make* them understand.

He turned his back on the sea and marched toward the upper ground, where the old trees leaned and shed their deep green shadows. And one thing struck him immediately. It had been spring in London, but it was full summer here.

He was almost into the wood when a huge butterfly flitted past him. And then another.

Apollo stopped. "I wish I had a butterfly net to catch them—those are beauties!"

What markings they had on their wings! They made him think, as the light caught them, of stained-glass windows.

He really itched to catch them. Then he could kill them and give them to his father to pin on a board, to make up for the cases the visitor had destroyed. Apollo had never hunted butterflies before, but the approval of his father had always seemed needful to him, for it was usually so difficult to get.

Just then, another of the butterflies flew right past Apollo, and he gave a yell.

The butterfly came back and hovered before him, as if to make sure he shouldn't be in any doubt.

It wasn't a butterfly, but a little pearly fish, and it had wings. The other two butterflies were also fish. Then Apollo saw that one was a fish, and the other a tiny woman with golden hair.

Apollo sat down without meaning to. After this, the fish-butterflies and the butterfly woman flew away into the shadows of the wood.

"I don't believe it," said Apollo. He knew he had just seen fairies. "Of course it's a trick. Probably clockwork toys. That's good. It means there's a house near here. I must keep a look out for it." That settled, he got up again and strode into the woods.

There is often something that feels uneasy about a deep wood, especially when you're alone and lost. But this wood had more of that feeling than most. It wasn't that it was ugly, or threatening, but it had an *ancientness*. Not only the trees looked old, but the smell of them, of their leaves and trunks, was old, and the light, which was so dark, yet green, here and there with droplets of bright green-gold, that, too, felt old as the trees.

Apollo marched on. This was quite hard, though. Roots grew across the ground from tree to tree, there were bushes and tall plants with white, sweet-scented flowers, and here and there a wild grapevine twisted around the trunks and branches. Also, Apollo began to sense that things were watching him.

"Of course, no one is," he said.

He turned sharply, and someone *was*. But it was only a nut brown squirrel. And the second time Apollo turned, it was only a dove, which cooed and flew away into the wood.

"I must get my bearings."

Apollo had been speaking aloud. He now heard someone laugh. He nearly jumped out of his skin, but then he realized he must be near the house he was looking for. He looked all around, but nothing and no one was to be seen.

Apollo decided to whistle. He whistled a tune that he made up as he went along. It wasn't very tuneful. Then he stubbed his toe on a root, nearly fell over a great rope of ivy, and heard laughter again. This time he looked right up. There, far overhead, where two trees met, he saw two girls' faces gazing down at him. Then they were gone.

"There's a rational—I mean. They had leaves in their hair. And no manners!"

Even so, he had the distinct idea they hadn't

had leaves in their hair. It was their hair itself which was lemony green.

At his school, Apollo was being taught Greek and Latin. He didn't like it much, which was actually the fault of his teachers, but no one had told him this. Through the writings of Greek and Roman authors, he had come across many myths. He had read about dryads, the nymphs who are each responsible for a particular tree and live inside its bark. He knew, too, that if a dryad's tree is cut down, she dies.

He was angry, upset, exhausted, scared—and very hungry. He heard himself shouting, "I'll get an axe, see if I don't. I'll cut down your trees and have them made into a table and chairs."

And from above there rose a thin cry of terrible fear.

Apollo scowled. He turned away. He remembered his mother saying he must always be polite to a lady, unless she were poor, or a servant, in which case she didn't matter. And then he thought, *Why didn't she matter if she was poor, or a servant?* And then he heard someone crying softly, and another soft, frightened voice whispering, "He doesn't mean it. He doesn't, dear."

The whole wood seemed to be listening then. Apollo had often been made to cry when he was very young. And he almost had, the first time Mr. Ruff caned him. (He *had* cried a little when the kites dragged him on and on through the air. But he'd made up his mind to forget that.) Even so.

"I say," said Apollo, looking at some pebbles on the ground, "I *didn't* mean it. Your trees are very nice. And I—I hate tables and chairs."

Silence. Then a rustle.

Apollo said, "Sorry, anyway."

He walked on.

Something hit him on the head.

Furious, he got hold of it and was about to start yelling about axes again, when he saw it was a large bunch of grapes, ripe and bursting with juice.

The dryads must have thrown it to him, to show how grateful they were. (Or that they forgave him.)

Only there were *no such things as dryads!*

Apollo gobbled the grapes, which were delicious and made him feel better. Obviously, they'd just happened to fall out of the tree when he was going past below, and the dryads—well, he'd sort of dreamed them.

He didn't find a house, however. Instead, after he had been walking for about two hours, the woods thinned, and Apollo came out on a wide pasture. It stretched away and away ahead of him, the grass sunburnt and full of red poppies. Then another wood began beyond it, or it was more a forest. Pine trees grew in it, getting darker and darker, and eventually climbing up the sides of the vast, double-white-capped mountain.

In the pasture there were long stands of trees, and Apollo thought that perhaps there might be a house among some of them, as he couldn't see any other houses, or a town, or anything civilized like that.

He therefore walked toward the nearest stand of trees. It was an outpost of the woods, and as he got into it, he found himself on a kind of natural avenue. And then he smelled a smell he knew.

"Horses."

Apollo had almost shouted in relief. He glanced to the left and right. On the left the trees were big and close together. On the right there was a high hedge of holly and juniper.

All at once a tall and hairy man was standing up on the far side of it.

Apollo stared at him and loftily thought he looked like a country person or peasant of some sort. He had a mane of hair and an *explosion* of beard. He seemed to be wearing a jacket also made of hair. He was very rough-looking.

He hadn't seen Apollo. Apollo drew himself up.

"Hey, you there."

The hairy man turned slowly. He had narrow

shiny eyes and a long nose. He blew through this and made a nasty puffling noise.

Apollo had thought the man was standing, but now he *really* stood up.

"Oh," said Apollo.

The man was unbelievably tall. Then, as he began to move, turning and coming out through a break in the hedge, Apollo heard the noise of unshod hooves on grass. Of course, the man was riding a horse.

"Well, my good man," began Apollo royally.

And then the man came right out into the avenue and Apollo saw him properly.

"Aaaah!" screamed Apollo. *"Aaaaarrrh!!!"*

And he whirled around and started to pelt back through the trees. But the man galloped after him, and inside half a minute, a huge hairy horrible hand had gripped Apollo by the scruff of the neck.

"And what are *you?*" questioned the "peasant," dangling Apollo three feet off the ground.

"I'm a boy," said Apollo, trying not to be sick.

"A boy? What's that? Do you mean a human?"

Apollo only gulped.

He knew what the peasant wasn't, and it was no use any longer denying it. He wasn't a peasant. To the waist he was a muscular and ridiculously hairy man. After that he became something else. He became—a horse. Man to the waist, horse afterward. Also hairy, smelly, and ungroomed, with four legs that ended in unshod hooves, and a long tangled tail full of burrs, twigs, and bits of grass.

"You're a centaur," said Apollo.

"So?" demanded the centaur belligerently.

"No, it's lovely," said Apollo. "Congratulations."

"Name's Klatter," said the centaur.

"How do you do?"

"What's *your* name? Got one?"

"Apollo."

The centaur kicked up his heels, neighed with laughter, and dropped Apollo in a prickly bush.

"Apollo is the sun god's name. You don't look like an Apollo. More like an Apolo-gy."

Apollo writhed, but said nothing.

The centaur, Klatter, slapped at a flea on one hairy horse side, then at a flea on his other hairy horse side.

"I've been out all day looking for something," said Klatter. "I suppose you're it. Come on, then."

"Er, thanks, but—"

Klatter hauled him from the bush. Klatter flung Apollo straight over his own, man's, head, onto his horse back.

Winded, Apollo lay there. And Klatter said, "Don't dare try to ride me. We're not to be ridden by you humans. We're better men than you are."

Then he broke into a mad gallop. Apollo clung on as best he could. The trees rushed by, then Klatter sprang out into sunlight again and through the high grasses. They were running toward the pine forest.

Apollo thought, *How I wish I hadn't climbed that rotten tree. It's all that girl's fault, that Hope Glover—*

Then the red flashes of poppies in dry grass were gone. The shadow of the forest fell on them. The wood had been nothing to this. Nothing had been anything—to *this*.

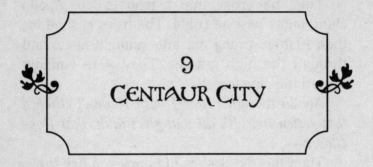

9
CENTAUR CITY

In the legends, centaurs had, frequently, caused trouble.

Apollo was soon remembering the Battle of the Lapiths and Centaurs, when a king in ancient Greece gave a feast, and the centaurs were invited. But the centaurs overate and drank too much of everything, and then started a fight at which people were killed and a war begun. Then there had been the incident with the hero called Heracles, who was having a quiet meal with some fellow, when the centaurs, smelling the food and wine, rushed in with torches and clubs, knocking everybody about. Also, Apollo thought, there was a centaur who had somehow poisoned Heracles—all told, you had to be careful of centaurs.

It was hard to think, though, while you were

being bumped along, lying the wrong way across a horse's back, and not allowed to ride it.

The forest was as dark inside as it had looked from outside. Now and then a spray of sun fell down through the pines. Otherwise it was like twilight. Sometimes birds called. Occasionally mice ran across the forest floor to avoid Klatter's pounding hooves. There was, too, the *noise* of Klatter pounding, and his snorting breathing on the steeper bits.

Then Klatter pulled up. A stream was running over pebbles, and the centaur leaned straight down, as a horse would, and noisily drank.

Didn't offer me any, thought Apollo resentfully. But then he wouldn't have liked drinking from the stream just after Klatter's beard had been trailing in it.

As Klatter was straightening up, there came another sound. This one was completely indescribable, but Apollo *tried.* He told himself it sounded like a huge rusty nail being twisted out of something smaller and even rustier.

"What was that?"

"What?" asked Klatter.

"That—*noise.*" Just then it came again. It was awful. "*That* noise."

Klatter shook water drops off his mane and beard.

"A bird."

"A—"

But they were off again, and once more Apollo had to hang on for dear life.

What kind of bird could have so appalling a cry? Klatter must be lying—but why would he?

How long the journey went on after that Apollo was unsure. It seemed like hours.

In the end he was so worn out by the unriding-ride, and being knocked breathless as he was bounced and thumped against the shaggy back, that he shut his eyes and more or less forgot what was happening.

When Klatter slowed down again, and when Apollo looked, the scene had changed.

They had come some way up the lower slopes, toward the mountain with the double peaks. Then Klatter had obviously gone down into a valley at the mountain's foot. The pines stood on three sides of the valley like a spiky black fence. Straight ahead they ran together and up the mountain. The mountain looked overpowering now. It was too big to see properly.

The little valley was green. A river ran through it, sparkling, and there were great boulders, some larger than a house.

"Get down," said Klatter. "I've carried you long enough, you heavy boy." And so saying he reared, and Apollo slid off his back—and straight into another prickly bush.

Once out of the bush, Apollo considered running away, but he didn't think he was up to it. Besides, the centaur was eyeing him closely.

"Walk in front," said Klatter. "Don't try to escape."

So I am *a prisoner,* thought Apollo. But he said, "Where am I to go?"

"Where I tell you."

"Where do you *tell* me, then?" Apollo was getting exasperated as well as worried.

Klatter sniggered. He sounded just like a horse sniggering, and Apollo realized he had heard horses make just this sound. Had they been sniggering at him, too?

"There," said Klatter. "Straight ahead."

Then Apollo saw that in one of the largest boulders was a hole. It looked like a tunnel mouth. It also looked most uninviting.

He walked forward and Klatter gave him a slap in the back. "Run!"

So Apollo had to run to the uninviting tunnel in the boulder, with Klatter trotting behind.

No sooner were they inside than the smell of horses became very strong, mixed with other, nastier, smells. And then there were two more centaurs in the way.

Although this was foolish, somehow Apollo must have been saying to himself that *one* centaur didn't mean that centaurs really *existed.* He must have, because when he saw the two new ones, he crumpled inside, and hung his head. Maybe he was just tired.

"Ho, Klatter, what's that?"

"Human boy," said Klatter. "Found it in the woods."

"Don't think much of it."

"No, nor do I, but it might be useful."

There were no introductions now. One centaur stayed in the tunnel. The other one, who had blondish hair, beard, and tail, and whose hairy horse body was a dirty yellow, pushed Apollo forward, while Klatter followed. Daylight filled the tunnel, then they were out on the other side.

Apollo saw something that made him think back to being very small, about three, and going out into a garden in the rain and making things out of mud. People had been very angry with him at the time. But someone seemed to have done the same thing here on a larger scale, and everyone must have been pleased. Because, waving his arm proudly over the huge shapeless lumps and mounds of dried mud, patched by grass, Klatter announced, "Centaur City!"

"Impressive, eh?" added the blond centaur.

"He's stunned by it, I expect," said Klatter. "Most visitors are."

"Oh, it's astonishing," said Apollo.

Between the mud things—they must be

meant to be houses or huts—ran grassy tracks. Here and there grew a tree, and in one place a stream went by on its way to the river. Otherwise, there was nothing of note. The "city" did go on for a great distance, though, almost as far as the deeper pines and the final slope of the mountain.

Apollo's heart felt hollow as it beat. If those were centaur houses, then there were a lot of centaurs here.

As Klatter and the blond one pushed Apollo on, he began to see some of these other centaurs. But there weren't so many. Then he saw, to his absolute horror, that several of them were *female* centaurs. The only real way to tell was because they didn't have beards—otherwise they were just a mass of matted hair and hairy clothes and twigs, with two arms and four legs, like the males. (One even had an old bird's nest caught in her mane. From the way she wore it, too, plaited in, you saw she thought it was decorative, like a fashionable hat, or a flower.)

When the females noticed Klatter and Basha—Apollo had heard Klatter say the blond centaur's name by now—they made shrill neighing noises that sounded scornful. Then the bird's-nest one came gamboling over.

"Ho, Klatter. What's that?"

"It's a boy, Hippo."

"It looks ill. Or do they always look like that?"

"Give it some grass," said Klatter.

"Do it yourself," said Hippo, and cantered off. She could be seen telling other females next, and they all went into peals of neighing laughter.

"Go on," said Basha to Apollo. "Eat some grass."

"Humans don't," said Apollo.

"I said they were stupid," said Basha.

"Go without, then," said Klatter.

Then they grabbed Apollo between them, one arm each, and ran with him through the mud city, showing him to everyone as they went. And everyone said, "What's that? Human? Useless." So that by the time they pulled up at an especially tumbledown mud-thing, Apollo was really past caring.

Klatter and Basha threw him inside. Apollo landed on a pile of filthy straw. And then Klatter and Basha pushed something big over the door hole, which closed it. Then they went away.

Apollo got out of the straw. (He had preferred falling into the bushes.) There wasn't much in the hut, though a hut must be what it was. Some greenish cut grass lay in a corner. It looked chewed. But there was an iron bucket full of fresh water and an iron cup standing by it. The cup and bucket weren't well made; they were lopsided. But they were recognizable human-type objects. Next Apollo saw some iron hooks in the wall, and off them hung six sharp arrowheads and a long knife with a ragged blade.

Apart from these things, there was nothing in the hut. Not even a decorative bird's nest.

Apollo went quietly to the doorway and tried to move the thing pushed across it. But it was made of pieces of tree trunk tied together with dried plaited grass. He couldn't shift it. And anyway, he could hear unshod hooves stamping to and fro outside, and now and then voices, though not what they said. Then there was a lot of raucous laughter.

Apollo sat down again, though not on the straw.

He tried to make a plan, the way intelligent young men did in stories. All he could think of, however, was that he was still hungry, and that he wished he was home—or even at *school*. And he wondered which dryad trees had been hurt to get the wooden pieces for the door blocker.

Then he fell asleep, and dreamed Hope Glover, the girl whose fault all this was, was wearing a silvery green dress with a mauve sheen on it, and she laughed and said, "Isn't this adventure wonderful?" And he wished he could shake her.

When Apollo woke, it was because Klatter and another centaur, who presently turned out to be called Hoofy, were shaking *him*. The door blocker was gone. Outside, it was getting dark, but there were lights.

"Come on. It's a party."

"Oh, good," said Apollo, feeling sick again.

"You're a real find," said Hoofy.

Klatter looked smug, and they pulled Apollo from the hut.

The centaur city seemed worse in the coming dark. Overhead, the light was almost gone, but stars were appearing, very bright. Here and there along the grass tracks, smoking torches burned on poles.

Klatter and Hoofy led Apollo through the city. Centaurs were now everywhere, hundreds of them, Apollo thought. Klatter and Hoofy were quickly joined by a Hod, a Bod, and a Thud. There were also a lot of big casks being rolled along.

In the middle of all the tracks and huts was an open space. At the center of the space a large fire was burning. The female centaurs seemed busy there, and Apollo now noted iron cauldrons hung over smaller fires, and he smelled what seemed to be burning bread, burning soup, and *toffee*—

Centaurs galloped about. They were all waving iron cups, and every so often they would swallow the contents, and then rush over to a line of casks standing under some trees. Here and there two or three or four centaurs were having a "friendly" fight. Hooves kicked and fists flailed. There were jolly cries of "You've knocked out another tooth, Bytis!" and "Tie their tails together, Horso!"

Then Klatter stretched out his arm and punched a large iron sort of gong that was slung from another tree.

Everyone stopped, and in the torch- and fire-light, a multitude of narrow crafty eyes turned glittering on Apollo.

"Here he is!" crowed Klatter. "My own discovery. Our little king!"

And then all the centaurs cheered and stamped, and Apollo was led forward, and he found himself being sat down very politely in an actual chair.

Into his hand they thrust a cup—not of iron, but silver. Apollo had the instant thought that both chair and cup were stolen.

"Drink, O little king!" warbled the centaurs.

Apollo realized he'd better—or better pretend. So he raised the cup to his lips. The smell of the drink was revolting, bitter and sickly all at once, but Apollo made out he sipped it. And the centaurs all clapped.

Then up came Hippo. Apollo noted that she had added a thistle to her bird's nest. With her was another female centaur who told him she was called Neigha. They gave him, on three badly made iron plates, just what he thought he had smelled, some burnt bread, some burnt vegetable soup, and not toffee, but burnt honey.

Long, long ago (yesterday, say), if strangers had made a fuss over him and called him king, Apollo would have accepted it, looking down on them yet not doubting they had every right to praise him. But he'd begun to think differently about a lot of things. He couldn't really think as he had before. Everything was altered.

Now he thought that in stories and legends, the hero was often tricked by flattery and by dangerous food and drink. The only contrast would be, in the tales, the food and drink had been irresistible. Despite that, Apollo was now extra careful to drink nothing (he tipped the foul stuff away whenever no one was looking, or he hoped they weren't—but they kept refilling the cup) and to eat as little as possible. That was easy, too; the food was disgusting.

But, "He likes our Ivy Brew. That's Ivy Brew in that cup, boy. Brewed from ivy, you know."

Most bothering of all, from the stories of centaurs Apollo had recalled, their most unpleasant behavior always seemed to be set off by feasts and eating and drinking.

Besides, he was their prisoner, surely, and one minute they were calling him "little king" and the next "boy," and, once or twice, "thing."

The more they ate and drank, the more loud and idiotic they got. They kept laughing, or neighing; they kept having fights, many of which were violent, if unskilled. Some of them sang, and they weren't good singers. Apollo thought it might be easier for him to get away from them if they kept this up. But however foolishly they carried on, they were all around him, and two or three, he finally guessed, were keeping a constant eye on him.

He thought, *This is the worst night of my life.*

And when he thought that, somehow all the other bad things, the other worst nights and worst days, seemed to shrink. Even his father, Mr. Rivers, looming over him, or Mr. Ruff with the cane, didn't seem that important.

Apollo thought, *Everything they told me anyway was rot. No such thing as fairies…and look at these centaurs. They don't exist!*

From the heat and fumes of the torches and fire, Apollo was falling asleep again, when Klatter gave him a light, but still quite painful, kick.

"Wake up, O king. Come and see the slaves."

What now?

But of course Apollo had to get up and go with them. All the centaurs seemed to be there still, milling around ("Pull your nose for you, Horso?" "Bite your ears off, Hod?").

As they came up among the pines again, the

air grew cooler and more sweet. And then there was a high, high wall.

Someone opened a tree-trunk gate, and Klatter roughly pushed Apollo through, saying, "This way, O king."

It was the oddest thing. After the noise and heat of the centaur's city, he found himself in a cool shadowy meadow under the stars. On the grass, things stood, which quietly raised their heads.

More centaurs? No. Now they really were horses.

"See," said Klatter, proud as anything. "Our slaves. Have you ever seen such beasts?"

"I—yes, I have. But they're—horses—they're like you."

"Like *me?* You watch your tongue."

"But—"

Klatter cuffed Apollo. Apollo was knocked flat. "Listen, king-thing-boy. We're better than horses, just like we're better than humans. See?"

Apollo decided to pretend again. "Oh, yes. Of course you are. Silly of me."

"That's right. Any being who has two qualities is better than one that only has one. Take Medusa, for example. A lady with snakes for hair. Got to be better than just *hair,* hasn't it?"

"Er—"

"Or the Chimaera, now. A combination of

lion, goat, and snake. *Three* qualities. That's most impressive."

Apollo said, "Yes, quite." But he was looking at the horses, who were slaves of the centaurs. They had lowered their heads again to graze, and the starlight shone on them. "So they're your slaves because—they're like you, but…inferior?"

"Got it. Oh, they're useful. They pull things along. Wouldn't catch us doing that. In the mines, for example, where we get our iron and stuff."

Apollo still stared at the horses. One in particular. This horse was a gleaming pure white. It looked like moonlight *made* into a horse. "Mines?"

"Where we get our metal, I said. The horses pull and carry. Even carry *you*. Can you ride?" demanded Klatter.

"Well, I suppose I can."

"That's good. Because you'll need to, tomorrow."

"Why?" asked Apollo cautiously.

"Young king like you—well, we're taking you up the mountain, birds-nesting!"

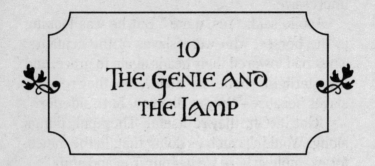

10
The Genie and the Lamp

About the time Apollo had been asleep in the centaur's mud hut, Hope was standing on the deck of the *Basset,* as the ship sailed up into the rainbow. And then she remembered the rainbow gloves she had left in the pocket of her maid's uniform, which she'd left in the cabin below.

The five dwarves stared, and so did the gremlins—there seemed to be about fifty of them on deck. "I won't be a moment—" cried Hope.

As Hope hurtled through the long corridors, dodging huge skulls and other curios of the inner *Basset,* she wondered what the dwarves would think now.

But it was the rainbow that had made her remember.

Hope flew through the door of her cabin, and instantly heard a frantic knocking. "Come in!"

she called. Then she realized the knocking was coming from *inside* her cabin. "Who's that?"

On the table where she had left it, the magic lamp from Sinbad's ship was jumping violently about. It wasn't someone outside the cabin knocking to come in—but the genie inside the lamp wanting to come *out.*

"Oh—just a moment." Hope dashed to the lamp and rubbed it. The genie burst from the spout so quickly it got squashed up against the ceiling. Its turban was crooked.

"I thought you'd never answer!"

"Well—I have. What's the matter?"

"Oh, you've no idea of the boredom. You must understand I've been cooped up for centuries in that lamp. I'm fed up with the place. I really must have something to do. Besides, I'm so out of practice. I need to polish up my skills." The genie sounded almost tearful.

"I'm so sorry. I didn't think."

"That's quite all right. Now." It adjusted its turban determinedly. "How can I serve you, O Mistress of the Lamp? *Three* wishes, remember."

Hope wracked her brains. She really wanted to get back on deck as quickly as possible. She was missing so much. Even as she ran off, the rainbow had been veiling the ship in all its wonderful shades of red, orange, yellow and green, blue, indigo, violet and purple. Now that she was

here she wanted to get what she had come for—
why not ask the genie to do it? That should be
nice and easy.

"O Genie of the Lamp," said Hope grandly, "I
wish you to bring me the rainbow gloves my
mother knitted for me...I know it's silly," she
added, "but if they're with me, I sort of feel she
can see the rainbow, too."

"No sooner said than—oops."

The cabin seemed to tilt over. The genie fell
down from the ceiling, and out of thin air burst
two rainbow-colored doves, made of wool, cooing
and flapping about.

Hope ducked the doves. The cabin righted
itself.

"Gloves," muttered the genie, "you said
gloves, didn't you?"

It waved its arms again and the two knitted
doves dived into Hope's dress closet. There was
a lot of scratching and cooing in there, but Hope
ignored it. She bent over her maid's uniform and
pulled the gloves out of the apron pocket. She felt
awful that she'd forgotten them. She had even
jumped on them.

"It's all right, honestly," said Hope to the
genie.

"Well, that's very nice of you," said the genie.
"Anyway. Let's try again."

"Do we have to?"

The genie blinked its yellow eyes. It looked awkward and anxious. So Hope said, "Er, I wish, please, for a glass of water." To her relief the glass of water glided through the air. She caught it, tasted it, and it was sea water.

"Something wrong?" asked the genie uneasily.

"No, it's delicious, only I do wish I could hurry and get back up on deck—oh! *No—no!*" Too late.

Hope and the genie were spinning through the air, along corridors, up and down stairs. Things rushed past and they barged into things which fell over, and one of which broke with a crash. Then, bruisingly, they whizzed up a ladder and out onto the *Basset*'s deck with a thump. *Embarrassing arrival number two,* thought Hope. *At least we didn't actually burst through the deck planks. I suppose I should be thankful.*

Hope picked herself up. Sebastian and Augustus were hurrying over, through rippling, incredible colors of light.

"Thank you, genie," said Hope.

The genie did seem happier. "Wasn't bad, was it? I haven't done anything like that since spiriting the Prince of Khalibarri out of the enchanter's dungeon—at least two thousand years ago. Now, your last wish."

"But I've had three."

"Oh, the ones that aren't right don't count," announced the genie. "Perhaps you should even have *two* more—that water was all right, was it? You're sure?"

"Yes, quite." Hope turned worriedly to Sebastian. "Perhaps one of these gentlemen would like the third wish?"

Augustus said, "Hrrr-umph," and seemed uncomfortable. Sebastian cleared his throat, then polished his spectacles.

Hope said, "Could I reserve the third wish for another time?"

"It's unusual, but why not?" said the genie kindly. "Yes. The lamp wishers are normally so impatient—give me this, give me that, now, now, now. It may come in handy, an extra wish."

All around, the rainbow distractingly bloomed. It was like curtains of colored water. Hope mumbled to Sebastian, "I'm *sorry,* and something—a vase, I think—got broken on the way up."

"I'm sure it can be mended."

"Are we really sailing upward?"

"Indeed we are."

"Oh, but look," cried Hope, "the rainbow's started raining." For shining flakes were floating down, now crimson, now indigo, now pale clear yellow like buttercups. "But—they *are* buttercups—and daffodils—and here come roses and carnations and peonies—bluebells—irises—"

And orange rain fell, and it was marigolds. Then came cornflowers, gentians, and, of course, violets.

Even green flowers fell; no one knew their names.

Perfumes wafted over the ship.

"Ah," sighed the genie, "it reminds me of the Paradise Gardens of the Great Caliph." Then it peered round. "I should be going back in; now where's my lamp? I keep a diary," it added to Hope confidingly, "of things seen and done. Thousands of blank pages, but I can write something in it, now."

"I think we left the lamp in the cabin, because we came out rather fast."

"It usually comes with me anyway," said the genie. It stared down to where its long tail of smoke now ended in nothing. "It must have come detached—never happened before—but I thought I felt a tug—"

Tulips and amaryllis fell. The genie smiled. "I'm out of the lamp, but it must be near...This means I can grant wishes without any wait, over and over!"

"Hrrmph," said Eli now, and wiped his forehead with his handkerchief. From the helm came a growling sound, which seemed to have something to do with Helmsman Archimedes.

"Please, genie, don't overexert yourself," said Augustus, frowning. "Have a little rest."

At that moment, HMS *Basset* crested the upward curve of the rainbow, and utter silence fell. Even the genie was silent. Even the gremlins.

They were high in the sky.

Hope stared. If she hadn't known, it might have seemed almost as if they were still below on the blue sea. But here the sea was sky. And when you looked over the sides of the ship, you could make out the real sea far, far down, with here and there the forms of islands, which now looked flat and misty, like artistic drawings of islands on a map.

The top of the rainbow bridge ran for quite a long way. And now that they were up here, she saw the rainbow was a field of flowers of every rainbow color and shade, each in a beautiful band, and all bathed in light.

Some way off across the blue sea of sky, clouds rested in a long line. They were on the same level as the *Basset,* and they were like islands, too.

Hope, when she had had time to watch clouds, which hadn't been often in the past seven years, had been fascinated by the different shapes they could take. These clouds, too, had shapes.

One directly across from them was quite marvelous. White billows rose up into cloud cliffs of gold, and on their heights were what looked like silver buildings of high walls and gleaming pillars.

"Now," interrupted the genie, in an eager voice, "if one of you wanted to wish, we could be over there, by that silver-gold cloud, say, in the blink of an eye—"

"No—no, thank you!" said Hope.

Captain Malachi approached. He looked at the genie and said, "The *Basset* makes her own course, sir." He sounded quite stern. "To interfere with that might bring about unforeseen difficulties."

The genie wriggled. "Well, perhaps I could just—"

"Oh, genie, please," Hope broke in quickly, "please—well...I wish you could straighten the ship's banner."

Because of the pulling wind from the rainbow, the silk banner was still all tangled up, and Hope thought that this might be a truly simple magical task. The dwarves, though, looked unhappy, and Eli took a sort of hopping step forward, then stopped. Hope began to wish she hadn't spoken at all. But it was again already too late.

The genie had waved its arms. The banner, with the ship's motto in gold letters, CREDENDO

VIDES, was now a writhing mass—

As everyone, including the genie, watched in dismay, the gold letters fluttered right off, tumbled over each other in the air, and were then propelled back onto the banner—which now stood out very stiff and straight, as if it had been starched.

Augustus covered his eyes with a groan. Eli hopped in one spot. From the helm bellowed the voice of Archimedes, saying something that probably it was as well no one could make out. Sebastian took off his spectacles, again rubbed them, and put them back on. But evidently, from his face, the banner still said what he had thought that it did.

The golden letters had reassembled wrongly. The *Basset*'s bold, inspiring motto now read: SEVEN DRIED COD.

Captain Malachi spoke very quietly. Everybody heard him. "Are you able to correct that, genie?"

The genie mumbled, "Your wish is my— um—I'll try."

This time the whole banner seemed to come upsettingly apart. Then it reformed once more, and still too stiff and straight. The golden letters had changed. They read: COD NEED DIVERS.

"Oh dear," said the genie. "This ship's magical, too, isn't it? That can cause problems, you see." And then, "Look, there's my lamp!"

"Perhaps," said Captain Malachi, "you should go back into it."

"Those gremlin things are playing with it. I wish they'd stop. Get back in? I'm not able to, you see. Not until I've granted three wishes. That is, I can *save* a wish, but not three…and once I've *started* to grant a wish, anyway, I have to keep on trying until I'm satisfied I've got it right."

"Oh, no," muttered Eli in despair. Augustus had taken out his tiepin and was chewing it. From the helm came another roar.

"And there goes the lamp," added Sebastian.

Everyone looked around and was just in time to see two gremlins shoving the lamp into a third gremlin's hat. It was the first time Hope had seen any of the gremlins look grim.

"My lamp," wailed the genie, "give it back—where's it gone? Oh—oh—I've lost all power. I can feel I have. I shan't be able to do any magic at all."

"Such a pity," grumbled Augustus.

The gremlin with the lamp in his hat now clamped the hat on his head very firmly. And the next minute he was away up a mast with five or six other gremlins.

It was now impossible to tell, Hope thought, which gremlin and which hat had the lamp. She felt sorry for the genie. And rather guilty, too, about the trouble it had caused, since it had come aboard with her.

The genie had coiled up on its tail. It was wringing its hands and moaning to itself.

Above, the undignified banner was still saying COD NEED DIVERS.

"I'm afraid this may be rather serious," said Captain Malachi.

Hope was frightened and looked it. She had got used to being blamed and punished for things. Malachi shook his head at her, and Sebastian said, "Don't be upset, Hope. It's not your fault. Such mishaps happen. However, in a way our ship gains her energy from the force of human imagination, and faith in dreams. *To Believe Is to See*. Now, apparently…"

"Now, apparently," said Malachi, "we carry a distress message from some fish. And as you'll notice, we have stopped moving."

Augustus, who had climbed a mast to the crow's nest lookout, called down to them, "An approach to starboard, Captain!"

All eyes now turned to the right side of the ship.

At first it seemed that the long gleaming cloud island had detached smaller cloudlets from itself, which now came toward them. But surely they moved too fast for clouds.

"It's a flock of birds," said Eli.

White and golden and silver-shadowy, with a beating of wings, the creatures flew nearer and nearer.

"They're very *large* birds," said Hope, still nervous. Then she caught her breath. "Oh—they're not birds at all. Look, it's a flock—it's a herd—of flying horses!"

11

THE CHILDREN OF PEGASUS

Over the air they came, their great shining wings spread wide. There were seven of them. They had all the noble beauty of horses, yet they were finer, thinner, and yet much larger, and they were wonderful dappled pearly shades between tawny amber and silver black. All but one. And he was white as snow and his great wings seemed to flame like the sun.

They circled the *Basset,* and from the wind of their wings, which smelled of sea and air and leaves, the sails stirred, and suddenly the banner loosened and went back into a proper shape. (Although unfortunately it still read COD NEED DIVERS.)

When something is entirely lovely and wonderful, and immensely powerful, clean, and good, it's possible to be afraid and yet not *fear.*

Hope couldn't explain what she felt any other way. She gazed at the flying horses, and when all at once they let their open wings rest, and the air currents bore them circling slowly, round and round, like giant gulls, she held her breath. And then the white one, who seemed to be their leader, drifted down as lightly as the rainbow flowers had done, and settled on the deck.

He folded his wings, and even so he was to a horse what a year is to a day.

And then he spoke. "I am Perichrysos, of the Sons of Pegasus. You are welcome. What is your errand in our sky?"

To her unease, Hope realized the dwarves weren't saying anything. And now the white horse with wings looked directly at her. His eyes were black and gentle. But his was the quietness of great force that never needs to show itself off.

"Maiden," said Perichrysos, "I see the errand is yours."

"Is it?" stammered Hope.

"Therefore," said Perichrysos, "we will escort you to our king and queen."

Captain Malachi bowed to the white horse. "Sir, our ship's becalmed. We can't move."

"I think you must wait for a fair wind," said Perichrysos. "In the meantime, the maiden shall come with us. It isn't our custom, you'll understand, to allow any to ride us, except as our gift to them. It's my gift to you then, maiden. Don't be afraid. Riding a winged horse, if one allows you to, is far easier than riding any other kind of creature. I will kneel down for you, and then you can climb up on my back."

Hope was dumbstruck. She didn't know what to do. In confusion, she looked around and grabbed Sebastian's hand. "There, Hope," said Sebastian, "it's nothing to be frightened of. *Believe* in it, that's all you have to do. And in yourself."

Perichrysos had kneeled down on the deck— he took up a lot of room. Even kneeling, he was magnificent, miraculous. He said, mildly, "Perhaps, little maiden, you'd be happier if your friend, this gentleman, came with you?"

Sebastian's face lit up, all the velvety wrinkles running like a wave of smile. And Hope whispered, "Yes, please. Will you, Sebastian?"

Sebastian bowed to the winged horse. As he did so, with a flourish, he doffed his spectacles, like a hat. It was somehow a very gallant and gracious gesture.

"Thank you, sir. I'd be honored. What a treat."

"Lionstar will carry you," said Perichrysos, and at his words, an amber horse swept down, found room for himself, alighted, and kneeled for Sebastian.

Both Sebastian and Hope, however, needed a bit of help. When they were seated just behind the arched necks of the horses, in a space before the huge wings began, Perichrysos told Hope to take hold of his mane.

"I don't like to," said Hope shyly. "It's too beautiful."

Then Perichrysos laughed. When he did this, the other horses also laughed. It wasn't jeering laughter, only amused. And—it sounded like neighing. In fact, if they had been anything but the wonders they were, it might have sounded rather funny.

This made Hope feel much less anxious. And when Perichrysos said, "Never be afraid to touch either beauty or ugliness, Hope. Never be afraid *not* to touch what is bad or wrong," she took hold of the snow-silk mane.

And then she grabbed it hard, for the next instant they were soaring up into the sky.

In seconds the *Basset* became tiny, as she had first seen it from the kite carpet. Colored ribbons of light were swirling up from the rainbow still, all around the ship. Presently these passed over the flying horses. And flowers fell again. They caught in Hope's fluttering hair and in Sebastian's flowing beard. On Lionstar's back he looked as excited as a child, and Hope lost all her own fear.

Now they were racing over the blue sea of the sky.

A flock of birds did appear just then, blue and pink birds that darted quickly away beneath the hooves of the flying horses as pigeons might have avoided a horse's hooves galloping on a road in the ordinary world.

Hope flung back her head. Happiness filled her, soaked her through. She began to sing in a high clear voice, a song she made up as she went along. It didn't make much sense, but no one told her to be quiet, or to "take her head out of the clouds," or that she "couldn't live in Cloud-Cuckoo-Land." How could they, she was *there!* And perhaps the blue and pink birds which had passed had even *been* cloud-cuckoos.

It was a glorious ride. It was like the best sort of dream, but it was real.

All too soon she saw the great cloud island approaching and others alongside and behind it. Then the seven horses dipped down.

The first clouds lay in the stillness of the sky, but at their feet, some tide of the upper air—a little wind, perhaps—creamed their edges like surf against a beach. Out of the billows of the cloud surf rose the cloudy golden cliffs, and from several of these poured white smoking waterfalls, but they were *cloud*falls. And on the clifftops there really stood wide courts and avenues and colonnades of pillars and buildings with great windows, and they were made of something that looked like silver and which shone. And on the nearest clouds there were gardens visible, too, each grouped about a walk—or flight—of open sky. But how could there be gardens up here? They had enormous slender trees in them, and the leaves of these trees glowed like bottle glass or garnets.

Perichrysos flew down into a courtyard, and Lionstar and the other horses followed.

The court was as large as a ballroom, and the floor and walls of it were a sort of marble. But it was cloud marble, though it stayed motionless and solid.

Half of the court was shaded by a rich translucent green canopy. But as Perichrysos trotted toward it, and then under it, Hope realized it was the foliage of another tree. Its roots were fixed in a single cloud that hung overhead, and the leafy branches trailed down over the court.

Presently they passed a cloud fountain playing in a pond of sky. Sparrows were diving through the pool like goldfish.

Then Hope saw that at the court's end, many more horses were grouped, hundreds of them, their wings folded. There was a long, golden seat, on which reclined, in an elegant way, one white horse and one black horse. But to say they were white and black, as Hope said afterward, was like saying the sea was just a bit damp.

The black horse, a mare, was like a starry night, and the white horse like the moon itself, if snow fell on it.

They were even more beautiful, and strange, than Perichrysos and his companions. And on their heads, between the ears, which on any other horse might have made them look silly but which on them seemed only right, were two golden crescents, like crowns.

The crowned horses turned and looked at Hope.

At her aunt's house and in "service," Hope had been expected to curtsy to all sorts of undeserving people, bad-tempered old ladies, foul Mrs. Crackle the cook, and heartless Mr. and Mrs. Rivers. Now, as Perichrysos kneeled again, Hope stepped from him, and curtsied perfectly in her long dress. And Sebastian beside her once more bowed.

It was Perichrysos who spoke.

"Your majesties, here is the maiden, Hope. And her friend, Sebastian, of the ship *Basset*."

Then the white King horse rose, and so did the black Queen horse. And as she did so, Hope saw that, of all the hundreds of horses in the court, she alone had no wings.

"My name is Pegasus," said the King. "Have you heard of me?"

"Yes, your majesty," said Hope. "Often. My mother told me a story about you."

"What did she say?"

"About how the hero caught you and tamed you and—um." Hope stopped. Then she went red.

And then the King laughed. His laugh was more like a man's. "That would be the story of Bellerophon, and how, having—er—*tamed* me, he rode me in his fight against the monstrous Chimaera. But you see, I allowed him to ride me in the fight. It was my gift to him, so he could win."

Hope said, "I know that now, your majesty."

"This is my Queen," said Pegasus. And he let out one silver wing, as if putting an arm around the black mare. "She is called Black Grass. These other winged ones you see here are our sons and daughters, and their sons and daughters, too, and so on through many generations. The Children of Pegasus and his Queen, Black Grass."

When she looked at the Queen, who had no wings, Hope felt if anything more amazed than when she first saw Pegasus. So she curtsied again, even more perfectly—it is sometimes possible, despite what is said, to improve on perfection.

Black Grass nodded. She said, "My lord the King chose me for his wife, and I him for my husband, long, long ago, in the Golden Age at the beginning of time."

"But how—" Hope stopped.

The Queen said, "How do I come to be up here, without any wings to carry me into the clouds? I'll show you, maiden, but not yet."

At that moment, on the mast of the *Basset,* uncountable wing lengths below and away, the banner writhed and rearranged itself from one last fragment of muddled magic. Two gold letters sprang right off it, and landed on the deck, where Captain Malachi, Augustus, Archimedes, Eli, and a collection of gremlins stared at them. They were an E and a D.

The motto now read: VERSED IN COD.

12
A BOY AND HIS HORSE

That evening, while Hope was on the cloud islands, walking through astonishing gardens and drinking nectar, Apollo had been in the centaur's unpleasant ramshackle "city." When Hope went to bed that night (in a cloud bed), Apollo was at the centaurs' revolting feast. After which he was shown the slave horses in the pasture with the high wall. And then he, too, went to bed, but in the hut, and with feelings of dread and exasperation, wishing very much he could escape—and thinking he probably couldn't.

The centaur Klatter had said they would take Apollo birds-nesting. A week ago, and in other company, Apollo would have loved this idea. Now he didn't. Frankly, he thought anything the centaurs did was probably going to be wrong, not to mention disgusting.

He slept heavily if uncomfortably. But when he woke, hot and covered in straw, it was to a most appalling din.

Apollo jumped up and ran to the door thing, which to his surprise was pulled partly open.

Apollo forced his way through, and then flung himself flat with a cry.

His first impression was that it was snowing or hailing huge whirling blocks of white and dark ice and snow. Then he realized he was covered in feathers. On holidays by the sea, Apollo had watched seagulls mobbing fishing boats, attracted by the smell of the catch. Were gulls attacking the centaurs' city?

The air was full of yells and roars and furious neighs. Apollo raised his head, and an iron arrow sped past the end of his nose to bury itself in the ground.

"Hey," said Apollo, offended. Then something hit him on the head, and he was lying facedown again, this time in some extremely squishy mud.

"This is too much," said Apollo, and he staggered to his feet, shaking his head to clear it, which didn't help much. He found he had reeled right into the blond centaur Basha.

"Here, watch it, you boy."

"Oh, excuse *me,* I'm sure."

The attack, whatever it had been, seemed abruptly over.

Apollo stared up into the morning sky. Some huge birds, white, black, or tawny colored, were lifting away very high up. One last feather spiraled down. It was enormous, strange, and rather beautiful. Apollo caught it in his hand, admiring, despite everything, its smoothness and strength. It was nearly as long as his arm.

"What birds were those? Was it the sort of bird I heard make that rusty sound in the woods yesterday?"

"Hold your noise," replied Basha charmingly. He plucked the iron arrow out of the ground and dropped it back into a badly woven grass bag on his shoulder. He was also holding a rough-looking bow, which he now gave a smacking kiss. "Trusty old bow, saw 'em off, eh?"

"Saw off whom?"

"Shut up, I said. That's your breakfast there, if you want it." Apollo looked and saw some burnt bread lying in the mud.

"No thanks."

"Please yourself."

All around, the male centaurs were cantering about, braying with apparent joy. A female centaur, the one called, Apollo thought, Neigha, was scowling and shaking an empty iron plate at the sky. (It occurred to Apollo she had been bringing him the bread and had just pulled the door half open when the attack began.)

"Oh, Neigha," said Apollo, "what birds were—"

"Weren't birds," said Neigha. "Are you blind, or what?"

Apollo gave up. As if for something to do, he started to pick up spent arrows, but presently another centaur careered past and snatched them from his grasp with a curse, aiming a blow at Apollo's already-sore head.

Would it be possible to get away? Apollo thought not. While picking up the arrows, he had been sidling along through the camp, looking for an escape route, but hadn't found one, and now anyway here came Klatter, with some of the others.

"Well, little king," shouted Klatter, "pretty good fight, eh? Saw 'em off properly, didn't we? None so brave as a centaur. No weaklings here."

"I was most impressed," said Apollo. (He thought he sounded like his own father; Klatter had sounded like his father, too.) "By the way, Klatter, what kind of birds *were* they?"

Klatter broke into rolls of laughter. Apollo saw he, and now most of the centaurs, were again all drinking great gulps of their repulsive Ivy Brew. He hoped they wouldn't offer him any, and they didn't.

Hod, Bod, and Horso had by now hemmed in Apollo.

"Ready for your jolly adventure?" chortled Horso.

"Mmn," said Apollo.

"Not a moment too soon," said Klatter. "That spot of trouble just now proves it. This little king I found, all on my own, he'll be the saving of us, mark my words."

And then Apollo forgot about the bizarre birds and even the birds-nesting, because untidy Hippo was trotting up, and she was pulling along, by a rope of grass, a pure white horse that shone like a star the night had left behind. The horse Apollo had seen the evening before.

"The king likes it," said Klatter. "Ought to. Best horse. I'm sure he's properly grateful."

"You mean I'm to ride *him?*"

"Of course. You're the king! I tell you, that white one, he's never even pulled a cart in the mines or carried a basket or bag. And look, Hippo's gone and groomed him and all, sentimental dope that she is."

Apollo had already noted, with horror, some spiky weeds plaited into the white horse's mane.

The horse stood there patiently, silently. Apollo walked up to him and the dark eyes looked deep into his own.

Apollo reached up and put his hand on the neck of the horse, firm but gentle. And the horse turned his head and looked at him again, then lowered the head in a quiet, noble way. Apollo stroked the long nose with its feel of prickly velvet. He muttered to one of the great, lily-like ears, "Don't worry, I'll get those weed things out of your mane." And the horse made a soft sound, as if he understood.

But this was a far bigger mount than Apollo had ever ridden. He had a feeling the centaurs had chosen the horse for him to try to make a fool of him. But Apollo knew that here was one thing he could still do well and take pride in. And before anything else could happen, he braced his foot against the horse's side, trusting him to stay still, now that they were introduced. Then he took hold of the mane and pushed himself up in a sort of leap, which only a good horseman can ever manage, to land solidly and neatly, and not too heavy, on the high white back.

The centaurs had watched. A couple made scornful comments, but they were halfhearted. They seemed reluctantly impressed.

The horse had a rough saddle of woven grass, which, next to badly made iron things, seemed the centaurs' next badly made favorite. Now Hippo gave Apollo the grass rope, which turned out to be part of a sort of makeshift halter and reins.

"Thought you'd fall off," regretted Hippo.

But Klatter cried, "What, the little king fall off?"

And then there was more yowling and bumping about as the centaurs got ready for their jaunt. Apollo sat on the white horse in the middle of it, stroking the weeds out of the white mane and whispering to the sensitive ears.

"I'll take care of you, horse. I wish you were mine." And then, impulsively, "When we're in the woods, perhaps we can really get away, you and I."

And Apollo had a sort of waking dream of riding through the countryside of this actually wonderful island, with its winged fish and dryads—which somehow, sitting on the horse, he really did believe he had seen—and long blue and green summer days of freedom, eating wild grapes and honey.

It was odd to think like that. It must be lazy and perhaps not manly. And there was school to consider, and the future—Apollo's *importance.*

"Off we go!" hooted Klatter, clattering up and slapping the white horse hard across the flanks to make him jump, but the white horse stayed steady.

The centaurs had moved in round Apollo, and they were leaving the centaur city—which also now seemed to be on the move. Horsy figures milled about, jars and sacks rolled (or got dropped), and the other horses, the "slaves," were there, hitched to carts or loaded with masses of centaurish junk.

Soon, however, Klatter's band reached the valley's upper end, where the pines drew close and the mountain rose over everything, pointing twice into the sky.

Once they were in among the trees, the centaurs' noisy mood changed. They became quieter, and also more sullen. They were passing something about between them, examining it. It looked like iron chains, but Apollo couldn't really make out what it was.

"This birds-nesting, now," said Basha on Apollo's left, "it's a very interesting sort of bird."

"Just an ordinary old bird, really," interrupted Klatter, to the right. "But the egg—well, now, it's worth having."

"Oh, yes," agreed Thud, pressing in from the back. "That egg—what an egg!"

"Just an old egg, mind you," added Klatter.

Apollo began to feel excessively uneasy. He realized, too, that though the centaurs had been all round him, now he, Klatter, Basha, and Thud had been squeezed to the front.

Pine shadows lay close and dark. The mountain was visible only in pieces between the boughs. It was much too quiet.

Suddenly there came once more that hideous rusty screeching Apollo had heard the day before. Only now, it was twenty times louder. And the centaurs all—*shied,* there was no other word for it. Even the white horse shook his head.

"What—" asked Apollo.

"Didn't hear a thing," said Klatter.

"Or," said Basha, slyly, "it might have been a winch in the mines."

"Our mines, winch, yes," said Klatter. "Got winches, pulleys. All modern conveniences. Inside the mountain, you see. We mine the iron and so on, for our arrows and knives."

"And chains," tried Apollo.

"Eh? Chains? What chains?"

Just then they came up on a rise, and the tree-line broke. The mountain swelled before them, vast in its icing of high snow.

The ground in front fell again, and through the pine trunks and strewn boulders, Apollo noticed three or four black holes that opened low down in the mountainside.

"See? Mines," insisted Klatter.

A line of about ten more horses had now appeared and were moving slowly into one of the black holes. Each horse had two large baskets strapped on it. There were also two centaurs with sticks. Next second, both used these sticks to beat the horses—who started and staggered faster.

"That's—" Apollo flared. He'd meant to say, "Barbaric and cruel, mean and stupid!" Someone else had said something very like that to *him,* and about *him,* but he couldn't recall who or why, and anyway Klatter and Basha, Thud and Bod were leaning near, glaring. "—so *clever!*" cried Apollo.

Hod slapped Apollo on the back and Apollo nearly fell off the horse. *And it serves me right,* thought Apollo, *for lying like that. But I can't do anything else, can I?*

Yet he knew the white horse had heard him. He felt bad.

They turned back into the pines, and soon they were climbing in a tunnel of trees and shadow. After about half an hour, this route led them in against a flank of the mountain, although its top was again lost to sight in the trees. Another little stream ran along here. Klatter called a halt and a midmorning snack—which consisted, for the centaurs, of more Ivy Brew and clumps of grass and clover, which they pulled up with their brawny arms and then stood thoughtfully chomping, fronds protruding from their beards.

Apollo dismounted and led the white horse to

the stream. Although the centaurs could see him, he was now out of their hearing, he thought. They were still unusually quiet. Perhaps they didn't want to scare off this bird whose nest they were so interested in.

"And I bet it *is* a strange one," Apollo murmured to the white horse. "Probably dangerous, too, some sort of eagle, like those birds that attacked this morning."

Then he said, even more softly, "I *didn't* think it was clever, you know. About the horses in the mines, and the sticks. I had to lie because otherwise they'd only thump me. And that wouldn't help anyone. I wish—" Apollo paused, but he meant it, so he went on, "I wish I could get all of you horses away from them. Set you free."

The white horse only went on drinking.

Apollo said, "I think I'll call you White Mane. That's a good name for you."

The white horse shook his white mane, and water drops flew up like diamonds in the shade.

Five minutes later, Klatter and Bod came over.

"See that rock, there?"

"Yes," said Apollo.

"'Round the other side you can get in under the mountain. Part of our old mine workings. If you go through, you'll come up onto the higher ledges."

"Where *it* is," added Bod, in a most sinister voice.

"This bird's nest, do you mean?"

"That's it. The *nest.*"

"Like to try it?" asked Klatter.

"Not much."

"We insist."

"Then I don't seem to have much choice."

"That's the spirit."

"Go on, then," urged Bod, and he lifted an iron knife and began paring his nails meaningfully.

"You mean I go in alone?"

"Oh, we'll see you *in.*"

"Kind of you," said Apollo, gazing at the uninviting rock.

"Don't mention it."

Once he was again mounted, about twelve of the centaurs herded Apollo around the rock. A cave gaped there. It looked dark and unwelcoming, like the other mine entrances he had been shown.

"How will I see my way?"

"Oh, light comes in everywhere. Most of the galleries are open. We abandoned—er, got bored with them long ago."

"Just keep going up," said Klatter. His eyes gleamed. He was a combination of eager and afraid, and full of ill will. All the centaurs acted the same way.

Apollo tapped the horse gently. "Go on, White Mane." And he rode forward and into the mountain.

Apollo looked back once. By then he was on a curving track, but there was a long gap far above, and dim light did come in. Apollo saw all the centaurs standing by the cave entrance, with drawn knives and strung bows. Klatter gave him a threateningly happy wave.

Then he turned the corner.

The way up was nearly all there was. There were no obvious side turnings that Apollo found, and no ways to get out, except if you went back. It seemed particularly frustrating to Apollo that he and the horse were now on their own, but had no means to escape. Perhaps when they came to the top? After all, if Apollo avoided the nest, the bird might ignore him. There might then be some other way to get down, out of sight of the lurking centaur party.

Light came in all the time, from rents above and in the sides of the rock. The mountain walls had been hacked for metal, and everywhere lay shards and stones. The path slanted up, and sometimes there were shallow terraces, which the horse managed well. Sometimes birdsong sounded from outside, and once or twice, Apollo could see over to the forest, now far below.

"I suppose," he said to White Mane, "we could just stop in here. They seemed frightened to come in, but there isn't any immediate danger. If we wait, they might go away—" Somehow Apollo didn't believe that, though. He and the horse went on.

Finally there were no more gaps, or only small ones, and the light more or less faded. Apollo didn't like this; it made the going trickier. Besides, the passage, or whatever it was, now kept opening out into great spaces of stone, and he could hardly see into them, and couldn't see where they stopped—or what might be in them. Some very peculiar shadows seemed to be moving in there, and weird echoes came and went. Even the soft footfalls of the unshod horse sent eerie sounds floating away and away.

"I don't like this much, do you?" Apollo whispered. But the echo took the whisper, and it, too, went circling around the stony spaces, *mush-mush-do-ooo.*

Apollo didn't speak again. He'd been going to add that there was beginning to be a very worrying smell. One of Mr. Ruff's masters had kept a parrot. This smelled like the parrot cage, or like two hundred parrot cages.

Then the passageway turned again, and then

once more, and suddenly the brilliant light of day poured in, blinding Apollo. He reined in the horse, and they stayed completely still until Apollo thought they could both see.

What Apollo then saw was this: an absolutely enormous step of white stone running up into the sky. On either side was an impossibly gigantic pillar made of what might have been black marble, and each of these was the height of—well, Apollo extravagantly thought, probably St. Paul's Cathedral.

Beyond, the blue sky shone, with the sun almost at its noon apex. And the peaks of the mountain hung directly above, blazing with sunlight and snow.

"That can't be a step. Or pillars. It just *looks* like—a step and pillars."

Apollo directed the horse to go on, and they moved along the base of the step, and then came out onto—

It was a huge space of floor, a floor that had been laid with an ornate pattern of green and red tiles. But each tile was the size of one of the houses in Cavalry Square.

"This is a giant's ruined mansion," said Apollo. There was no echo here, and he forgot to speak softly. "Or, part of one—why not? There are dryads and fairies and centaurs, and so a gi—"

The horse shivered, and the next moment the

air was split right down its center by the most
ghastly and deafening *screech*. It no longer
resembled a rusty thing turning in a smaller,
rustier thing—it sounded as if a side of the world
were being torn away.

Apollo flung around in the saddle and almost
slipped from the horse. What he saw somehow
kept him on the horse's back.

The floor stretched away behind them, too.
And there in the middle of it was what looked, to
Apollo's bulging eyes, like an actual, human-size
house, made of carved and gilded wood. But at
the top of the wooden house, something sat,
which had perhaps been dozing quietly in the
sun but now had woken up and stared at him
with eyes of liquid fire. It was the *bird*—but the
bird wasn't a parrot. Nor an eagle. If only it *had*
been.

It was so large that, so very large that—in fact
the bird, too, was about the size of one of the
tiles—it was the size of a *house,* or just a little bigger.

It was black in color, with a burnt-gold sheen
on it, and its beak was like cut topaz.

But its eyes blazed on Apollo, and then it
shifted upward, and spread out one of its mighty
sooty wings, and he saw that it had indeed been
sitting on a huge white egg—*that* was only the
size of the Riverses' dining room!

To make matters worse, Apollo realized just what the bird was.

Though he would never have admitted it to his father, he had read the *Arabian Nights*. So he knew all about the adventures of Sinbad, including Sinbad's two meetings with these terrible furious razor-taloned birds. The bird was a roc—and it hated all things but its own kind.

And of course now the roc was standing right up. With a horrible graceless *hop* it sprang off its nest in the wooden thing, and landed there on the giant's floor. Not for one instant did it take its eyes from Apollo. And then, rather than screech, it *hissed* like a snake.

Apollo turned and frantically kicked his heels into the horse's sides. *"Giddy-up—Go! Go!"* Howling this, he grabbed the grass halter and also the mane.

At once the horse shot forward. But even as he did so, Apollo heard the astonishing noise of the roc lifting into the air. The red-hot wind of its wings swept across him, nearly knocking him right off the horse's back, while its shadow, short from the high sun, flooded over them. And in that shadow he and the horse were very, very small.

Apollo—who would never normally have kicked a horse, and would have punched another boy who did so—now kicked again, and now they were racing across the enormous floor before the shadow of the roc.

And then Apollo saw, too, that a few feet ahead of them, the floor ended. It ended in bright blue sky, at the edge of the mountainside.

If he could have pulled the horse to a stop he might have tried to do it, even with the roaring hissing shadow right behind them. But it wasn't possible to stop now, riding full-tilt as they were.

Apollo clung to the horse's neck. "I'm— sorry—"

And then the floor slid away and there was nothing beneath them, except a mile of sunny empty air, and the hard ground far down at its bottom.

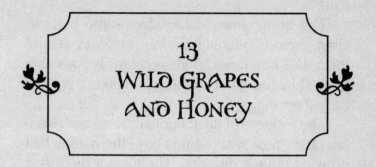

13
WILD GRAPES
AND HONEY

For what felt like forever, Apollo kept his face pressed into the mane of the white horse, and clung to the strong white neck. Then it suddenly seemed to Apollo that something hadn't happened that should have by now. They should have hit the ground. They hadn't.

Then he made himself open his eyes and sit back a little to see. It took a lot of courage to do that. But when he had done it, Apollo's mouth fell wide open with surprise.

They were dropping quite fast, but not as fast as they should have. Instead of falling, in fact, they were—*gliding*.

"Oh, horse," breathed Apollo, in respectful wonder.

And even as he said it, the horse veered again a little and slid away to the left, and then again to the right, sinking down and down, but diagonally.

The horse was *coasting,* like some big, circling pigeon, catching the air currents, letting them drift him down. And somehow he was able to do this, the horse, although, unlike a pigeon, he had no wings—

The terraces of the mountain, some with leaning pines, now towered up above them; they had dropped quite a distance. The tops of the forest were near, and then Apollo saw the dazzle of the river, a wide stretch of it. He understood the horse was letting the air currents bear them over toward the water.

There was, though, one other thing. High above in the noonday sky, the rook-black roc was also hanging on the upper airs. It didn't hurtle down at them, but Apollo could see it was watching. It would probably wait, Apollo thought, to make sure they landed far off from the egg—and then attack. He could remember vividly how the rocs in the story had bombarded Sinbad's ship with stone, and sunk her.

Just then the horse caught some powerful downdraft, and they were soaring, almost diving, in toward the river.

Apollo yelled as pine branches speared up at them, catching at the horse's tail, then mane, and at his own hair. Then they were rushing straight through the crest of the pines, and in the next second hit the surface of the river with a violent glittering splash. Their speed continued to rush them forward, and the water was carved up on either side of them in two great silver waves—as if, now, the horse really did have wings. And then everything grew steady. The horse was only swimming strongly for the riverbank.

Drenched from head to foot, buffeted, bruised, and shaken, Apollo slipped from the horse's back to leave the animal free. They swam separately to the bank and scrambled out, and in that moment, behind them, the roc, now deadly silent, came catapulting from the sky.

Apollo was sure he heard its talons rip the surface of the river as he and the horse fled in among the pine trees.

Then there was only running, and stumbling over roots and fallen tree trunks, and panting for breath, with the sunlight flickering on and off between the trees like yellow lightning. Soon the horse was far ahead and Apollo ran alone. He thought he could hear the shrieks of the roc, but distantly, and then he was no longer certain.

At last Apollo tripped over one more root and fell prone, and couldn't get up for a while. He lay there on the thick moss, and smelled a lovely scent, which came from a bush of flowers near his face. And he heard only his gasps for breath, and then nothing. That is, he heard grasshoppers and crickets and bees and birdsong, and a whisper as a little gilded snake rippled by through the fern. Nothing else. When he sat up, the white horse stood after all nearby, peacefully cropping the grass.

The forest had changed again. Now it was a wood mostly of ancient oaks and beeches, and the light which dappled through was golden green and bronze.

Between the columns of the trees Apollo saw a deer leading her fawn. They paid no attention to Apollo, or to anything. Nothing harmful was near.

He got up and went over to the horse and pressed his face into the pale neck.

"Thank you. I don't know how you did that—it was as if you could fly—it was magic, wasn't it? Even the roc seems to have lost our trail...How wonderful you are, White Mane."

Then the horse spoke.

"That isn't my name."

"You—can talk!" Apollo burst out laughing. It was disbelief, but also delight.

"Yes, I can talk."

"But you didn't before."

The horse said, "You were close, with the name, though."

"What is your real name?" asked Apollo

humbly. "I'm sorry I got it wrong. Sorry about kicking you. And the mountain. Everything."

"You were the first to ride me," said the horse. "We're not to be ridden, my kind."

"*Oh—*"

"However, let's say it was my gift to you."

"Thanks," said Apollo, even more humbly. "It was a marvelous gift. And you saved my life."

"My name," said the horse, "is *Light* Mane."

"Then I nearly *was* right—almost—"

The fawn and the deer had vanished through the trees. On a bough above, a heavy honeycomb hung out, the golden honey dripping from it. The surrounding bees moved calmly, showing no annoyance at Apollo or the horse.

Then a butterfly went dancing past.

"Look—a fairy—"

But it *was* only a butterfly this time, and that made Apollo laugh again.

"I wonder why the roc didn't keep after us? Surely it would have, it was so angry."

"Something else has distracted her," said the horse. Its voice sounded more human by the minute. "Too late, no doubt."

"What do you mean?" But Apollo had just found a wild vine curled around the tree. The grapes were purple and onto them the fresh honey had dripped. He snapped off a bunch and began to eat hungrily.

"The centaurs in the valley," said the horse. "Once they captured the wingless Children of Pegasus, they tasted power over others. They keep such horses as slaves. Not just to help them in their mines—where they hardly ever work in any case—but because they have, those centaurs, the need to feel superior. Best of all, they'd like to storm the cloud palace of Pegasus himself, and take captive the horses who are *winged.*"

"But winged horses would fly away," said Apollo. He added, "Like the ones this morning that attacked the centaur city. They were *horses*— horses with wings—" But then he returned hungrily to the grapes. The horse's voice sounded peculiar—perhaps because it was going on so. But Apollo wasn't really listening.

However, through his munching he heard the horse say, "No, the winged horses, once captured, would be as much slaves as the wingless kind. Klatter and his band would clip their wings. Like the wings of tame ducks."

At that Apollo raised his head. "But that would be—"

"The centaurs in the valley have everything worked out. Klatter and Basha thought of the plan long ago. But they were much too cowardly to put the plan into action. Then you came along. You were very useful."

"Me?"

"You were the decoy, meant to lure the roc away from her egg. Klatter and the rest had always been too scared to do it. While you distracted the roc, they climbed up by another route—the mountain is full of chambers and passages—to the nest in the ruin. They had an iron net, and by now they will have got the roc's egg safe into the mine workings. The roc is far too large to get through the narrower passages. The wider ones they'll have blocked up."

"I don't see—"

"They will tell the roc their terms. Either she helps Klatter's centaurs to storm the cloud islands, or the centaurs will destroy her egg—or so they will say. On the other hand, if she refuses them, they have the egg and can hatch it. Then the new roc will be their slave, too. She perhaps seemed to you, the roc, to have no brain or intelligence, but her instincts are strong and she can understand very well. Then again, the winged horses can be terrible in their own way in a battle. Do you know about Bellerophon and the Chimaera? This is going to be a fearful business all around."

Apollo stopped eating grapes. "But, Light Mane, if you knew all this—why didn't you say something earlier? Why did you just carry me to the nest and—and help make their plan work?"

"Light Mane didn't know the centaurs' plan.

Light Mane has only just realized, as you have, what you've both done."

Apollo spun around, since obviously it wasn't the horse who had been talking all this time.

Another centaur stood among the trees. He wasn't like Klatter or Basha or Horso. The long black hair that covered him was clean and combed like satin, his beard was trimmed, and his mane and tail were plaited tastefully with green vines. Even so, he was a centaur—and there were others, four or five or six, grouped behind him.

"Now look here, you fellow," began Apollo, having had about enough, and standing up straight.

But just then there sounded again the frightful screams of the roc. They were deafening, and terrifyingly close. The centaurs looked up but did nothing else. Something tore by, raking the topmost crown of the trees. The sunlight exploded, and broken twigs and leaves fell down. Squirrels leapt from bough to bough, chattering with alarm. One more long, raucous cry went trailing over, thinned in distance, and ended, seeming to leave a shaking hole in the air.

Everyone waited. Afternoon sunlight settled, the minor noises of the woods came back.

The dark centaur paced over to Apollo. "That cry was full of pain. They've taken her egg, we can be sure of it." Then he held out his hand in a gentlemanly way. "I'm Oaken. These are my brothers. We keep to ourselves. We find the horses with wings never trouble with us—we're literally beneath them. As for our cousins in the valley, Klatter and his mob, we're as unalike as flint and fur. You and the white horse are welcome to come to our camp."

Apollo made a decision and shook the centaur's hand. For a moment, shaking the hand of a being half man and half horse, the boy heard the voices of his father and Mr. Ruff buzzing in the back of his head. Apollo felt how important he was, a human, who wore proper clothes and would one day make money and have power in the world. And then he thought what a *fool* he was. "I'm Apollo Rivers. Thanks, I'll be glad to go with you. Is the camp far?"

When they reached it, the centaurs' camp lay beside the river, at the edge of the trees. It was full of sunlight, and smelled of woodsmoke and the clean groomed scent of horses. There was laughter, and someone singing to the reedy thread of a pipe. Then Oaken and his brothers trotted in with the boy and the horse, and heads of long, burnished hair turned to see, and flower-decked tails flicked with curiosity.

Of course, Apollo had heard of good centaurs, the centaur Cheiron, for example, who had been a teacher and healer. Were these centaurs more like that?

It seemed they were. Soon Apollo was sitting on a log, and two foal-centaurs, a little girl and a boy (giggling and nudging each other at Apollo's "odd" appearance), had brought a polished wooden plate with warm slices of bread, shelled nuts, ripe figs, and a drink of sweet grape juice in a clay cup.

"But where does this wooden plate come from?" Apollo asked, thinking of the dryads and their trees. The foal-girl said, "From a fallen bough, of course. We'd never *cut* a tree."

Oaken sat not far off, near the fire, with a gingery centaur called Bay, and Oaken's sister, Quickfoot, whose ash-blond hair was plaited with columbines.

"Oaken, where's Light Mane?"

"Eating clover. He hasn't had any for a long time. Klatter and his band keep theirs all to themselves. And it will do him good, poor Light Mane. He was distressed, realizing how he'd helped with Klatter's plot."

Apollo glanced around. Despite the roc, and everything, he had the sudden dreamy thought that it would be wonderful here for long summer holidays. Not for always, perhaps, because he would want to be doing something, too. Now his father's voice and Mr. Ruff's voice were silenced,

Apollo wondered for a moment what he really *would* want to do. But then Bay spoke up, and Apollo's thoughts scattered.

"I just met Thorn. He says some of the winged horses have been flying around the mountain peaks. The roc's disappeared, gone into the mine galleries maybe, until the way gets too narrow for her."

"To lose her egg—" said Quickfoot. "Every mother's worst fear."

Apollo said, "Can't anything be done? To help the flightless horses, I mean."

Oaken shrugged. "It seems unlikely. There are always these fights. It's better to keep out of them."

"We keep to ourselves," added Bay.

The other centaurs by the fire were shaking their heads. "Get involved in someone else's trouble—before you know it, you're in over your hocks."

Along the riverbank, some of the foal-children were playing. Two had pet squirrels and one a pet snake, and these ran or coiled about, joining in the game. A fish jumped in the water.

Oh, hang it all, Apollo thought. *They're not bothering. And I've had enough for now.*

The plate was empty and he put it down. He leaned his back on a sun-warm tree, and closed his eyes.

14
THE MAIDEN

The night before, in the cloud islands, had begun gloriously well. First of all, Hope and Sebastian were invited into the great gardens of the sky.

They sat among trees and even banks of flowers that hung down or grew upward from rafts of cloud, while cloud marble fountains gushed rain and petals.

It was explained that moisture was stored in these clouds, renewed with every rainfall. The plants were nourished by this. The seeds of the plants had been brought from lands below, but the trees and flowers had changed as they adapted, becoming more slender, and partly transparent. Their leaves were edible and the winged horses sometimes grazed on them, but only enough to prune them. Otherwise the horses drank nectar, a golden beverage of the gods to which they were entitled, since they, through Pegasus, were related to the god Poseidon.

Hope and Sebastian, as their guests, were allowed to drink nectar, too. It tasted delicious, and seemed to do them both good, but one tiny cup was almost too much, and then you wanted nothing else.

As the day ended, the cloudy gardens turned to breathtaking rose reds, saffron, and pink. When the sun had quite set, night spread like a deep blue wing, and all the stars came out in its feathers. Stars also fluttered alight in King Pegasus's trees.

"Are they real stars?" Hope asked, because she had been told that *real* stars were vast balls of fire, like the sun.

Queen Black Grass answered, "Of course those stars you see far off are indeed the suns of other worlds, just as your teachers taught you. Always remember, not everything that is said to be real is false. And even a bad teacher can teach you things, if you are patient enough to do half their work for them. However, there are other kinds of stars, and some of those are here. A wishing star, for example—would you like a star to wish on?"

Hope was so astonished she didn't reply. Sebastian said mildly, "Sometimes silence speaks louder than words, your majesty."

Black Grass rose and blew softly up into a tree. At once a little star, about the size of a moth, came flitting out. It was exactly the *shape* of a star, the way everyone draws a star, and it gleamed. Hope opened her hand and the star flew onto her fingertip. But she couldn't think what to wish for, and after the genie she was half afraid to. No one told her off or sneered at her when she said nothing, and the little star took off again, back into its tree.

All this time, King Pegasus and his Queen had spoken generally, about the islands of the clouds, the gardens and trees, nectar and so on. But as the darkness gathered, and soft cool winds blew through the sky (at which the stars in the trees tinkled like bells), all the horses seemed to drift peacefully away, flying and walking, leaving Hope and Sebastian alone.

Then Hope, who had been puzzled for a long while, said to Sebastian, "How is it that they speak English, as we do?"

"Oh, but they don't," said Sebastian. "Nor do I, my dear."

"Then how—"

"On the *Basset,* as in the Lands of Legend, anyone can speak any language and be understood by everyone else. This is the country of imagination, and imagination, you see, is a language common to all."

Through the dark trees, the glimmering winged horses moved to and fro. The moon was rising, and the silvery walls of the palace glowed.

Then Perichrysos, the white horse who had let Hope ride on his back, was there, beside her.

"The King asks for you," said Perichrysos. "Come, maiden."

As he turned and walked away, Hope glanced at Sebastian, but she was still used to doing what she was told. She followed Perichrysos.

They went up through the gardens, up into the silver courts, up to what seemed to be the highest court of all, above the palace. The moon burned, and hundreds of winged horses had gathered in the court, gazing at the moon. It shone in all their eyes. How unbelievable all this was—yet she was here.

King Pegasus now stood before her. At once he spoke.

"We have expected you," said Pegasus.

"Me?"

"For many years. You, or one like you. We have always believed that if a human came to our islands, he or she would be our friend, because of the bond between your kind and ours, formed so long ago, when I helped Bellerophon."

Hope's mouth had dropped open. Then she remembered the horrible boy Apollo, standing with his mouth open, and she snapped it shut. "Your friend…"

"One who would help us."

"Help *you*—but—"

"We're at war," said Pegasus gravely.

There was a vast sigh, all around them. It came, not from mouths, but from a rustling of wings.

"And after all," said Pegasus, "you are well-omened. You are called *Hope.*"

Hope simply stared. She was so astonished she only felt numb.

"Maiden, the hour has come when I must tell you of the war between my kind and the centaurs in the valley of the mountain. It comes about because they enslave those of my people who are born without wings. Not all the centaur race is bad, though they are doubly creatures of the earth, and therefore strange to us, who live in the sky. But the centaurs in the valley are that terrible combination of witless and wicked. They spend their lives squabbling and fighting, drinking and eating. They hate anything else, yet neither do they like their own kind very much. What they fear most, however, is that which is the most like them—yet *unlike:* horses, and mankind."

Hope had sat on a bench. She was listening, spellbound, forgetting her own part in the story.

Pegasus told her how the flightless horses spent most of their time on the land, or by the sea (for they, too, had the divine blood of Poseidon, the sea god). They had, though wingless, an ability to use the updrafts and air currents about the mountain, but seldom did so. They preferred the firm ground under their hooves, or to swim, to circling and floating in the sky. But for this reason, the centaurs had been able to catch them, grazing on the sea island below.

When this had happened, Pegasus had sent word to the centaurs, but they rudely refused to talk to him. The centaurs said that Pegasus was a *horse,* and couldn't talk, just as the wingless horses couldn't, though naturally they could. The centaurs had also declared that not only would they never free the horses they had taken, but they would one day find the means to invade the sky islands above. Then they would kill or capture the flying horses, and Pegasus himself, and clip their wings, and work them in the mines.

While Pegasus was saying this, some of his courtiers grew restless, raising their wings with great feathery sighs of sound, their moonlit eyes flaming. When Pegasus finished speaking, the amber horse, who had carried Sebastian to the sky, stepped forward.

"King, let twenty or ten go with me tomorrow.

We'll attack the centaurs' filthy huts. Humble them and tear them with our teeth, break their bones with our wings—"

"I forbid it, Lionstar," said Pegasus in his grave voice. "In the past such attacks have done nothing. These centaurs make weapons, and some of you will be hurt. That's happened in the past also."

Lionstar tossed his mane and the moon in his eyes burned red.

"If you forbid me, sire—I must disobey."

Others had come up behind him, fanning their wings, pawing the cloud floor of the court so it churned like boiling milk.

Then the Queen was there. She arrived in an amazing fashion, sailing up from the palace wall, borne by a night wind, in the magical way Pegasus had said was possible to his wingless children. Pegasus must have gifted this magic to her, for in fact, Hope saw, Black Grass used the wind, then somehow had no need of it—she had stopped quite still in the air above them, her legs curved up and in, almost like a cat's. She was ebony black on the white round of the moon, and on her forehead her golden-crescent crown was the shape of a mysterious smile.

"Don't let's make war, too, among ourselves," said the Queen. "There's no need for this. Look, there is the maiden, there she stands, the human we've waited for, who will save us."

Hope seemed to feel a million eyes blazing on her, and over all, the huge eye of the moon. And then she did the most awful thing she had ever done in her life. She gave a thin wail, like a baby, and turning, she ran away. Down the steps from the high place, which seethed with anger, sorrow, eagerness, and moonlight, down into the gardens. She ran and ran until she bumped very hard into something that went "Ooph!" and then she found she had knocked Sebastian over, just under a crimson tree of staring stars. So she covered her face with her hands and burst into tears.

Sebastian, it seemed, wasn't one of those people who shout at you when you cry (*or* knock them over), or who tell you they'll give you something to cry about, or to pull yourself together, as if you were in bits and all the bits were attached to pieces of rope. Nor was he one of those people who throw their arms round you. He only stayed very still, and sometimes he patted Hope's arm very gently. He was patient, knowing crying sometimes takes time. And when Hope cried less, he handed her a snow white handkerchief with the initial S in one corner.

Hope wiped her eyes. "What have I done? How *could* I? What will they think of me?"

"Perhaps they thought you were frightened."

"That's terrible."

"Why? Don't be afraid of being afraid. How can you be brave if you're never afraid of anything?"

Hope said, "I'd have to be brave to go back and explain. And I will have to. Say how I can't do anything—and say it to all those shining horses!"

"But are you sure you can't?"

"Oh, Sebastian—they're kings and princes and gods—and they seemed to expect *me* to help them. They said so. In a *war*—but I don't know anything at all—" finished Hope desperately.

Sebastian said, "You know a lot of things."

"Nothing!" Hope was in despair. "I'm just a girl who can only be a maid-of-all-work in a house in London. A maid—not a maiden! What use could I be here?"

Sebastian watched the moon with his kind old eyes, but then the moon filled both lenses of his spectacles, and he seemed to wear two white moons instead of glasses. He said, "You didn't make a wish on the star. What would you *wish* to do? After all, the genie can't hear you!"

"Poor genie! I wonder if that's why so many things we wish for go wrong. Are there genies somewhere, trying to grant our wishes but making a mess of it? And that's like me, too, because I do want to help the horses so—but I'd make a mess of it."

"Well," exclaimed Sebastian, "look there!" He

pointed at Hope's feet. Where some of her tears had fallen, nourished by the additional water, a new flower had grown, a pale silvery pink. "Sometimes," said Sebastian, "it's just a matter of carrying on as if you *do* know what to do. Just pretending, and believing."

"I don't believe in *myself*," said Hope. She faced the courts of the palace. "I'll go and tell them," she said, "that I can't. I'm not the person they're waiting for. How could I be?"

It did need bravery. She walked back through the gardens, and climbed the stairs, up and up to the high place. She was trembling, but when she came there, not one of the flying horses remained. Even the moon had gone over. There were only shadows in the court.

A frightening idea caught at Hope. If she didn't believe in herself, how could she believe in her dreams—could she even believe in the *Basset,* or Sebastian, or Pegasus the King? And if she didn't—had they ceased to *exist?*

Then she saw something lying on the ground, which shone. She went over and found it was one long, tawny golden flight feather. Hope picked it up, and when she touched it, she remembered again the wonderful ride through the sky on the back of the horse called Perichrysos.

If such a thing could happen, wasn't it possible, too—just possible—that she, Hope Glover, the little nobody—that *she* might be the human maiden the Children of Pegasus said they needed so badly? Why else was she here? After all, her tears had grown a flower.

Not quite knowing why, Hope pushed her hand into her pocket and touched the gloves her mother had knitted. Wouldn't her mother have *loved* this place? And if her mother had been telling Hope this story—if Hope had been the story's heroine—Hope's mother would never have said the heroine's answer was—No!

Suddenly a thrilling excitement poured through Hope. She lifted her head to the starry sky, and all alone in the courtyard, she cried: "Then I will! I will help you! Even if I don't know how."

Only silence answered her, and yet it rang like a great cheer.

And then a little winged foal came trot-fluttering up and announced it was a page of the King's. It led Hope away to a bedroom with a cloud bed in it, a guest room made specially for a human guest. Hope asked anxiously if Sebastian had a cloud bed, too. The foal assured her he did. Then Hope asked the foal in a tiny voice if she had made King Pegasus angry, when she so rudely ran away.

"Oh, humans never behave as you expect," said the foal, closing the door with its wing.

I'm certain he was *angry,* Hope thought. *But never mind. Tomorrow I shall offer to do anything I can. And somehow it will be all right.*

And before another thought could come to spoil that one, she fell asleep.

15
LIONSTAR'S REPORT

When Hope again appeared before King Pegasus, she was wearing another new dress from the *Basset.*

It seemed the ship had moved again in the night, blown by the winds of the stars. Now the vessel stood like a golden toy in the sky bay below the cliffs of cloud. After three foal pages had brought her the dress, a red apple, and a cake—sent with the compliments of Captain Malachi and Eli—Hope looked wistfully down from her high window to the bay and the ship, wishing she were back on board. (Had the banner recovered? she wondered.) But then she ate the cake and the apple, and put on the dress. It was a long white one, gathered in the style of Classical Greece, and with a sunflower yellow drapery—out of which there came wriggling two gold things that fell on the floor.

Hope picked them up. They were two letters—a gold E and a gold D. "Why, they look just like the lettering on the *Basset*'s banner—"

She was quite right. This was exactly what they were. The E and D which had fallen from the motto CREDENDO VIDES. Evidently, the banner *hadn't* recovered.

She put the letters away into a handy pocket in the white dress; although Classical Greek dresses didn't normally have pockets, this one seemed to. (She had already transferred the rainbow gloves to it.) Then she went out to meet the King.

The sun was now very high, and she saw she had lost a lot of time in worrying, and also in preparing the speech she felt she had to make. But when she reached the flying horses' meeting court with the large tree in it, she found everything in confusion, many horses bounding over the clouds, flapping their wings, and calling out fierce sentences she couldn't quite hear, while other horses galloped to and fro. The crowd in the court kept going now this way and now that. While Hope floundered in the middle of it, trying not to be knocked over—the horses didn't seem to see her now—the sun climbed even higher. It was noon. Then Pegasus himself flew straight down—as it seemed, out of the sun—and as he closed his wings with a colossal clap, silence fell and motion ceased.

"Step forward," said Pegasus in a stern, cold voice. Hope felt a tremor of dread. Was all this fuss about *her?* Was he going to single her out and lecture her in front of everyone, as so many others had?

But before she could take a step, a group of horses galloped out into the space that had formed about Pegasus, flaring their wings and snorting.

"End this show," said Pegasus. "You disobeyed me. That's enough."

"Sire," said a silvery black horse, "our disobedience sprang from our love for you and for our wingless brothers. This morning we attacked the centaurs' mud huts they're pleased to call a city. How can you deny us the joy of such a skirmish?"

"What did it achieve?" asked Pegasus, gloomy and magnificent, turning his head away from them.

"Sire—it showed them—"

"What?"

"That we're powerful, that they've invited our rage—"

"Did you rescue any of your wingless brothers?"

"No, sire. It wasn't possible. It never has been."

"That then is my answer. But were any of you harmed?"

The silver black horse said nothing. The others ruffled their feathers. Then a gray horse spoke, "Lionstar, who led us—your majesty, we lost him in the fight."

Pegasus flung up his head and next his whole body, rearing. Against the sunlight his mane flamed like white fire, his wings gusted like winds. His hooves were terrible.

Then he dropped down and stood like a stone, and like a stone he asked, "Is Lionstar dead?"

"Sire, no—we *lost* him—not dead—he flew off and vanished. We looked—"

Hope would have done anything in that moment to ease the awful sorrow in the King horse's face. She pushed through the others, careless now of the huge hooves and thrusting wings. She went out into the space, and going up to Pegasus, she curtsied.

"Dear King, I'm so sorry. Is it my fault?"

"Yours?" Pegasus stared at her. "No, maiden."

Hope's carefully planned speech was forgotten. She spoke in a clear voice, and strongly, so they all heard her.

"I don't know what I can do, lord King, but I'm willing to do whatever I can. It will be an honor."

And then there was a great rumbling rushing sound below, and every one of them looked down into the air, where the winged horse Lionstar had just appeared below the palace, on wheeling pinions. He soared in and landed the next instant, with a huge clatter, in a shower of his own shed feathers and with seventeen or so rusty iron arrows spilling from his tail and mane.

"King Pegasus—I must report urgent news!"

"Do so, then," said Pegasus.

Lionstar shook a last arrow from his mane, and spoke.

"When the centaurs drove us off, sire, I took the opportunity to fly to the walled pasture where they pen our brothers. I meant to wish them courage. But none were there. Already they were out in the vile centaur city, on their way to the mines. As I was inside the pasture and unseen, however, I overheard two of the centaur women talking outside the wall. They were grumbling about having to pack things up, and I learned this: The centaurs captured a boy in the woods yesterday. It seems he's human, but he has the name of the sun god, Apollo.

"Now you'll remember, sire, a roc has recently come to nest on the mountain, in the ruin of the Titan's house. There is the fearful Box there, and the roc chose to make her nest in it. It seems she has an egg now."

"That may be bad news for us in itself," exclaimed the silver black horse.

"It's worse news still. The centaurs, having caught the human boy, are going to use him as bait to lure the roc from her egg. While he distracts her they will steal it, and will use the egg as a hostage to force the roc to serve them. We know they have a plan to storm these islands. With the roc to assist them, they can do it—or, if she won't, they will hatch the egg themselves and train the newborn bird to do what they want. They grow fast, as we know, roc hatchlings.

"As soon as I might, I got away to tell you— but there was great activity among the huts. They were all off to hide in the mountain until the roc was subdued. By the time I managed my departure, the kidnappers were well away on their mission."

"Are you wounded?" said Pegasus.

"A scratch or two, no more."

"Is it likely they can steal the egg?"

"Yes, sire, they have an iron net. Once inside the mountain, the roc will find the ways too narrow, and must bargain."

Pegasus said, "You, Snow Wing and Night Eye, fly down and see what's happening. Don't go too close. The roc is savage and never any friend of ours."

As the two horses lifted away, Hope saw

Sebastian standing with the Queen. The Queen said, "This is a dark hour for us."

Hope knew, from the *Arabian Nights,* about rocs. But she was also amazed at hearing that horrible Apollo Rivers was somehow here—and with the horrible centaurs. *Well,* Hope thought, *he would be.*

"If perhaps we are to be attacked by the roc," said the Queen quite softly, "and by centaurs carried on her back and claws, then our visitors from the little golden ship must leave at once."

"Yes," said Pegasus, "so they must." The day before he had laughed like a man. Now he sighed like one.

"But you wanted me to help you—" cried Hope. "You must let me try!"

"The time is past for that," said Pegasus.

Hope's heart seemed to drop like an icy boulder into the pit of her stomach.

If I'd spoken sooner—

Was it all her fault?

And what Box was it that Lionstar had talked about? The Titan's house—why did that sound so familiar?

"Perichrysos, Melanippos, will you see the maiden and her companion, Sebastian, safe to their ship?"

Hope said nothing, and now Perichrysos came over to her, offering once more the gift of his back to be ridden. The first time had been a flight of sheer happiness. This must be a journey of utter shame.

But as they dashed up into the intense blue of the sky, a rush of delight filled Hope anyway. She raised her head, burning with the only emotion she had left—*belief*. For they were, after all, *flying*.

And then she knew. "Perichrysos—that Box Lionstar mentioned, in the Titan's house—did the Box have anything to do with Pandora?"

"It did. She let out of it all the woes of the world."

"I *thought* it was. Pandora's Box—"

"How it came to the mountain I can't say. Some have it Pandora's descendants used the Box as an ark to save them from a great flood, and it washed up at last on the mountain... But if so, some of her husband Epimetheus's house seems to have come with it."

Hope thought, *The story I told Cassandra in London that day was Pandora's. The story I know best. So, though I don't know what it is, the answer is there—and this adventure really must be mine.*

"Perichrysos—please don't take me to the ship. Take me that way, down to the mountain, where the Box is."

"Maiden, the centaurs may still be there; at

best they are in the caves and mine workings. And the roc will be about, raging and dangerous."

"Then you must be very quick and fly away, because I can hide. Perhaps I can even find that Apollo and stop him—though I expect it's too late. But oh, Perichrysos, please."

"If you truly wish it, I will."

"I do, Perichrysos."

Then the great horse blazed white-gold as he turned in the air, and spun toward the island on the sea below, like another star to wish on.

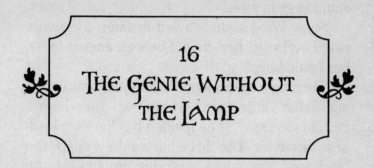

16
THE GENIE WITHOUT THE LAMP

The roc, not surprisingly, was Hope's first concern. But as they descended toward the island, passing through some last veils of thin cloud, it—*she*—was nowhere to be seen.

Instead, presently, a pair of winged horses came flying toward them from behind the two crests of the mountain.

"Snow Wing, Night Eye," said Perichrysos, "what news?"

"Everything is over, for now. The centaurs have the egg, and they're in the mine. The hut city is empty; they took our wingless brothers into the mountain, too. As for the roc, she flew around and around in a frenzy, until she found a way in at a cave mouth, but she can't go far. She's inside the mountain in the galleries of the mine."

It was black Night Eye who spoke, wheeling about Perichrysos.

Snow Wing added, "Even through the stone, twice we heard her cries. She's an enemy to us, but I pitied her."

Then they asked why Perichrysos was carrying "that little girl" down to the island. Perichrysos said, "The maiden has her own business to see to." The three horses drew apart, the black and the white swerving up toward the clouds. Perichrysos continued to descend.

In half a minute more they glided in around the white peaks, then drifted lightly as a single feather to a terrace more than three hundred feet below.

Hope sat a moment on the winged horse's back, getting her breath. They hadn't been lost on her, the dismissive words of the other two horses. But Perichrysos had spoken of her still as the maiden, and made her sound important.

When she thanked him, it wasn't only for the gift of the ride.

"There's time to change your mind," said Perichrysos.

Hope was also afraid there was, so she said quickly, "My mind's made up. Thank you again, Perichrysos, and please fly away before anything bad sees you. Give my love to Sebastian, if you can—" Then she felt like crying again, so she slipped very fast from the horse's back, and stood away to allow him room to take off.

He turned and gave her one look before he did so. It was a very gentle, searching look, the way animals sometimes look at humans even in the ordinary world. Then he nodded and the huge wings clashed upward, and in a leap like a white thunderbolt, he was into the sky, grew tiny, and had gone.

Hope was entirely alone.

The afternoon sky had become hazier, a yellower blue, and the heat was overwhelming. Hope glanced around to find some shade. Doing this, she took in properly for the first time that she seemed to be standing in the middle of a huge floor tiled in an intricate pattern. About a quarter of a mile off, or so it looked, two vast stone stems, like pillars, went up. Between Hope and these pillars was only one thing that cast a proper shadow.

She was in the ruin of the house of the Titan (those then *were* pillars, and that great bank between must be a *step*), and the thing that cast the shadow, the thing like a wooden house carved all over and gilded but without windows—

Was Pandora's Box.

"It's true," said Hope. Then she felt something she would never have felt in the ordinary world—*silly* for *not* believing that *anything* extraordinary was real.

At that precise instant there came a shriek from close by, yet inside the mountain. It was the most awful sound. It was ugly and menacing and savage, and it rasped on her nerves so she could hardly stand it. Yet at the same time it was so full of distress it was just as unbearable in another way. It was the roc, crying after her egg.

"The poor thing," said Hope.

And then all compassion left her, for the roc came shooting right out of the mountainside, out of some cave or other hole just large enough to provide her an exit.

Hope did the only thing she could think of. She fell flat on the ground and gripped the huge tiles with her fingers, and stayed as still as if she were part of the floor.

The incredible black shadow of the roc swirled over. And the dire smell of the roc, fiery and meaty and now poisonous with rage and hurt, almost stopped Hope's breathing.

But then the roc was high up into the sky. With one last desolate shriek, she plunged off toward the west. Unable to penetrate the mountain, it seemed she had given up her egg, as birds who are robbed sometimes do. At least the centaurs didn't seem to have persuaded her yet to attack the cloud islands—she had flown in another direction. But of course they would have tried, and she might come back.

So for a long time Hope lay facedown before she dared sit up and look around. When she did, the sky was quite empty. Then Hope got up and ran straight for the Box, and into its shade, to hide.

Like the ruined house of the Titan, this adventure seemed all too big for her.

"But I must try. I must."

Hope stared up at the side of the Box. Perhaps she could find a way to climb it? Then what? Inside it would be full of the remains of the roc's nest—and magic. It must be brimful of that.

Of course, there was no sign of that boy Apollo. He'd helped the centaurs, probably wanted to and enjoyed it. Now he'd be with them, showing off and thinking how clever he was.

The sun was moving to the west. The afternoon grew yellower and drowsier, and then the sun was lower and the sky more mauve. A salt-cool breeze rose from the sea that lay, dimly wrinkling, far below the mountain. All shadows were long now. Hope still sat by the Box of Pandora, thinking and thinking, knowing she had wasted yet more time, and unable to come up with any idea at all.

The roc hadn't returned and it looked as if she wouldn't. But soon it would be sunset, and

then night. It would get colder, and these shadows would take on disturbing shapes all their
own. Just as that one, there, over there, look, on
the white giant step, just as that one did already.
Because what threw that shadow? Nothing did.
Yet there it was. It wasn't a shadow—but it *was*
uncoiling, like a smoky snake, and now it was rising up and eddying along over the tiles toward
the Box, and in its darkness two pale eyes were
gleaming—

Hope jumped up, and as she did so, the snaky
thing bundled itself up in the air like blown washing, and then it flopped down a yard or so away,
and it wailed, "Forgotten again! You forgot me.
Left me. But I finally found out where you were—
I can tell these things, if I really put my mind to it.
And after all, you *are* the Mistress of the Lamp.
At least, I suppose you are, seeing those gremlin
creatures have hidden it, and all those dwarves
will say is *Hrumph!* And all these wishes I *insist*
you really must start to have, or at least order,
since I can't grant them yet—otherwise I won't
know where I am. Where am I?"

"Genie," said Hope.

"Oh, yes. Command me!" cried the genie,
quite aggressively. It seemed exasperated.

"But," began Hope.

The genie collapsed again. It lay there like a
burst balloon. "No, no, why should you. What's

the use? I did everything wrong. And anyway, without the lamp—I'm powerless."

Hope didn't know what to reply. Then she told the truth.

"But it's nice to have your company."

"Oh. That's kind of you to say." The genie reinflated slightly, sitting up and straightening its turban. Its pointed teeth showed briefly in a sad smile. Then, "But I know you can't mean it. I've only caused you trouble. And even the dwarves, how I've tried their patience. But do tell me," it added, brightening, "*if* I could grant you just one wish—what would it be?"

Obviously, even in failure, the genie was obsessive about its work.

"You're sure you can't?" Hope asked uneasily.

"Impossible," said the genie. "But anyway, if you could—just say it as if I could…you know, 'I wish—'"

Hope thought. She said, "Well, what I'd wish—all right, I *wish* that you could have all your magical power, even without the lamp, and all your old skill, so you could use it perfectly."

"What a shame," said the genie. "You see, that would have been the only wish I couldn't ever have granted. Since it would be for me. And, too, where anything's magical to start with, that always causes complications."

They both sighed.

Just then the sun sank deep into the far-off sea. Above, the stars burned up like struck matches, and over the sky one seemed to fall, like a single drop of quicksilver.

And now it'll get dark, Hope thought, *and I still don't know what to do.*

A shower of laughter, in two female voices, broke across the dusk.

How strange, it sounded familiar—

Hope turned and saw two young women in white dresses that seemed sprinkled by stars. They were walking briskly toward her.

They had pale veils—no, it was their hair. And they were both wearing the *same* dress, or both dresses were exactly alike.

Hope saw who they were. It was Cassandra and Miranda, the ladies she had first met in the house in Cavalry Square, at the start of everything.

"Hope!" exclaimed Cassandra. "You *are* here. How are you?"

"Oh—hallo—quite well—" gabbled Hope, puzzled.

Miranda, looking as queenly as ever, drew herself up. "Now, are you actually *you,* Hope? You're certainly part of my dream tonight, as Cassandra is—"

"We sometimes dream of visiting the *Basset,*" explained Cassandra, "but we haven't seen the ship yet. She's here somewhere, of course. We're on a mountain, aren't we? Just look at that lovely big golden star—"

"Even if you're dreaming," suggested Hope, "I think you're still somehow here."

"Oh, good," said Miranda. "Though I always think I am, when I do. If you see what I mean."

"When we wake up again," said Cassandra, "we can never be sure if we *did* visit. That's part of what I wrote to Sebastian about. In the letter I gave you, Hope, for him."

"Then again," said Miranda, "as we're all having the same dream, apparently, no doubt we can compare notes tomorrow. For example, both you and I, Cassandra, are wearing the magic dress."

"So we are! Isn't that clever. But how I wish," said Cassandra, "that Sebastian *were* here. And all the dwarves from the *Basset.*"

The genie, which had perhaps been looking for an opportunity of introducing itself, towered up in an alarming way. "Your wish is my command!" it gallantly squawked. Then it blushed blue-black. "Ah—my apologies. Forgot I couldn't—"

The interruption was very noisy. Over on the giant step, which still gleamed in the dusk, there came a sort of soft bang, followed at once by a great scuffling and tumbling and one long furious bellow.

Figures were rolling over and along the step, saving themselves, jumping up and down.

"It's Sebastian!"

"It's *all* of them—even Archimedes," said Miranda, "who looks *very* put out. And even a couple of gremlins, too."

"They must have hung on to the captain's coattails," said Cassandra. "That's why they've just landed on poor Eli!"

Hope thought both Cassandra and Miranda seemed more skittish than she remembered (particularly Miranda), but then people often were, in their dreams. In any case they were all hurrying over the long floor toward the tall step, where Archimedes now heroically stood roaring that it was a wonder the helm hadn't been wrenched off, the speed at which he had been pulled away from it without warning.

Hope stopped running and turned to the genie.

"*Did* you?"

"No, I can't have—"

"Cassandra wished, and then—here they are."

"Yes, but..."

Above, the sky was navy blue. The golden star shone large and bright, and beyond it, just faintly visible, was a luminous line of clouds that didn't move. Was the star the *Basset,* anchored below the cloud islands?

Stars and clouds—but what had put the genie right, and *without* his lamp?

"Perhaps," said Hope, firmly, "you should try something else."

For once, the genie hesitated.

"Oh, er, but..."

"I wish," said Hope, and paused. What did she wish? She didn't after all quite dare to wish for anything to do with the centaurs, the roc, or the Children of Pegasus, just in case. But perhaps there was one thing the genie might now be able to do that would help Hope organize her thoughts, and find the part she had to play in all this.

My part, she thought. *Yes, like a play. But look, the floor is like a huge theater set, and the step is like an upper tier of seats. Besides, the dwarves are up on it, and we down here can't get up on it at all.*

Suddenly Hope was full of—well, of hope. And with hope came bravado, and a host of extravagant notions.

"I wish, O genie, first, that we are all seated in comfort—no, luxury—on the step, and wait—wait—that we have with us a beautiful supper hamper, with—oh, what did the Riverses have?—cold salmon and salad and fruit tarts—and Stilton cheese—and some wine—and glasses of cut crystal and plates with a red and gold pattern—"

The genie blinked, looked as if it were going to sneeze or scream, and Hope rushed on:

"—velvet seats, and green curtains with silver tassels. And then—genie, I wish we can all see the story of Pandora and the Box, but out here, like a play in the theater. So we're not involved and no one gets *hurt.*"

The genie didn't sneeze, or scream. It spread its arms and its squeaky voice swelled up in a glad shout—and now it was like the voice of someone who has just recovered their voice after a bad cough, and it got stronger on every word. "I hear and I OBEY!"

Everything flickered for one brief second. There was no confusion or noise. They were merely there, seated, the dwarves, the two ladies, (even the gremlins, to their obvious amazement), Hope, and the genie itself, on the step of Epimetheus the Titan. They were also on little velvet chairs and had little gilded tables, and there was the very large hamper, spilling out the cold supper in an orderly way, and a bottle, out of which the cork was just flying with a *pop!* And before the step, in front of them all, were two tall pine trees leaning in together from the mountain-sides, to make curtains of black-green, festooned with silver tassels.

"What a glorious dream," said Cassandra.

Wine poured into a glass and floated to her hand.

"Perhaps it's all right," muttered Archimedes, accepting salmon. "I must be asleep at the helm. I should wake up, though, at once."

"See the play first," said Captain Malachi. "A long time since I saw one of those."

"The play's the thing," said Bosun Eli.

Seaman Augustus studied a wedge of Stilton. "Did some acting myself, once, in the Plunwijitt Isles…"

The hamper had wafted loaded plates even to the gremlins. They shoved the food quickly in their stovepipe hats, looked pleased and satisfied, and settled back all attention.

Hope glanced once at the sky. Only stars. Stars to wish on—somehow she trusted that if the roc returned, it wouldn't be just yet. Besides, you often had to go on with something or other hanging over you. The hamper had given her a crystal thimble of wine to sip.

Then the silver tassels unlooped by themselves from the two pine trees. Their heads sprang straight and there, in all its original detail, the house of Epimetheus was re-created, glowing with the sunlight of a Golden Age, although the evening stars still burned above.

17
ON THE STEP OF THE HOUSE OF EPIMETHEUS

Pandora wasn't that pretty, not really, not when you saw her. She had something, though, for which there has never been a name. So, despite her rather long nose, and her rather weak chin, and her ankles, which weren't entirely slender, and her hair, which was tar black rather than black silk—you looked at her, and you wanted to be her best friend, her *slave,* or, in the case of Epimetheus, her husband.

The house was another thing entirely. It was—*gigantic.* Vast pillars of black-and-red marble stretched up into a far-distant beamed roof, but the beams seemed made from the boughs of living trees, giant oaks or cedars, and foliage clustered on them, and sometimes little birds flew through the room and out at the huge, glassless windows. As for furniture, there were carved chairs, each as big and tall as a palace, and several chests, some like railway stations. In corners stood slender black jars with scarlet patterns, and these were only as large as the fountains in Trafalgar Square in London. There was also a bed behind a long white curtain on golden rings. The rings were bigger than cart wheels, the curtain was hundreds of feet long, and the bed was itself like a flat-topped mountain.

Luckily, the step they were sitting on had nothing to do with the doorway. (It led apparently to an upper story, where things were stored—a sort of attic, Hope supposed.) The luck about the door was related to the fact that the first thing they saw was Epimetheus entering through it. And Epimetheus was in his Titan form.

He looked like another column, not much recognizable as a man, and that was all Hope could really make out. Something so colossal was difficult to take in. Not until Pandora appeared, and Epimetheus shrank down and down until he was only the size of a large-boned man about seven feet tall, did Hope see he was very nice-looking and had fiery bronze-colored hair.

The beginning of Pandora and Epimetheus's marriage was nice to watch, happy and funny, as they tried to please each other, Epimetheus shy and charming, and Pandora seeming shy, but really, Hope thought, *sly.* (Now and then the pine curtains would close, as in a play, at the end of each scene.)

Then the Box arrived. The audience on the step didn't see it brought—any more than they had seen Pandora brought, which must have happened before the "play" began.

The Box was just there at the beginning of a scene. Against Pandora and Epimetheus-at-human-height, the Box was house-size. (Although to Epimetheus-at-Titan-height, it had only been like one of the smaller chests.) He had kept the Box, they learned, stored upstairs in the early scenes, but Pandora had recently said, Oh it was so beautifully carved, it would look much better in the living room.

So there it was.

"Shall I shrink the Box down for you, Pandora?" asked Epimetheus, still eager to please her. "I can do it the same way I shrink my own height." Then he seemed to think better of that. He muttered, "What's in the Box would shrink, too. That might cause problems." Besides, Pandora seemed not to have heard the offer. She was saying, "Why, it's exactly as high as the ladder you made for me that leans up to our grapevine." By which you could tell she had already cunningly measured it with her eye.

"Yes, Pandora, so it is. But never, never climb

up the Box. The lid must always stay closed. My brother, Prometheus, made me swear never to open it."

"Nothing," declared Pandora, wide-eyed, "was farther from my mind."

After that, however, things went on in the way Hope knew from the story.

Epimetheus had to go out. Pandora was alone. At first she kept circling around and around the Box. You knew she was up to mischief and you wanted to stop her, or at least dislike her—but you couldn't. She was Pandora.

Sebastian whispered to Hope and Cassandra that it was only with the greatest difficulty he stopped himself from going forward and offering to fetch her the ladder! While Hope knew, if she had walked into the scene, she would probably have climbed the Box herself, if Pandora asked. Pandora truly had been a very dangerous lady.

In the end she darted out and pulled the ladder into the house. She leaned it on the side of the Box, kicked off her jeweled sandals, and began to climb.

When this happened, all the little birds on the high boughs stopped singing. There fell a deep silence, like a shadow.

They had to watch Pandora reach the lid, and undo the lock with the large brooch she lugged from the top of a nearby table. The lid rose easily, for bad things so often happen very easily. It fell back with a crash, and Pandora leaned over and craned into the Box.

Her scream was awful. Hope felt sorry for her.

Then the whole of the Titan's house went dark. It was a most dramatic effect. In the darkness there rose a weird whirring and buzzing and scraping, and a vivid glare washed up from the depths of the Box.

Hope noted that even Miranda had clasped her hands together, and Captain Malachi clenched his fists. They all stared in revulsion, except for the gremlins. *They* were now hiding under their chairs. They had good reason to.

The Evils of the world were flying up out of the Box. Hope couldn't have named them—each and all were like nightmares come to life. They had tusks and fangs and claws; cold or burning, slitted or bulging wicked eyes; spikes, slithers, or steam for hair. Their breath was venomous vapor; they carried dreadful weapons—whips and cleavers, needle-like blades, cloths that flamed and dripped. Some had tails, and they could sting, for they lashed Pandora as she clung to the carving of the Box, yowling. They *grinned,* but without any humor. Through all their foulness, they looked, too, wretched and grim. They had been made to want to escape and cause harm, and yet perhaps they would have preferred not to. They would have preferred to have stayed prisoners in the Box.

On their dragonish wings the creatures flew about. Sometimes they came quite near the step, where the footlights would have been in a theater. The audience shrank back. But Hope had so wisely wished that the story be a *play* and that no one be hurt—it wasn't possible for the wicked things directly to reach them.

When they had investigated all that giant room, scratching at the furniture, tearing the curtain, spitting into the jars, the swarm gradually flew out into the world beyond the house.

They went one by one, and as they moved into the twilight that had, before their escape, been broad day, the dire, wordless cry of thousands of voices rose from the unseen land.

"How terrible, terrible," murmured Eli.

Archimedes said, "A dismal day, indeed."

The gremlins had completely vanished under their hats. As the last Horror flittered, batlike, into the gloom, Pandora still clung tottering on the ladder. Then Epimetheus appeared, only seven feet tall, in the doorway.

"Pandora—what have you done?"

"I couldn't help it!" Pandora whined. "I can't help making trouble. It's how I am." And then to her credit she began to cry.

But the light was altering. Subtly, slowly, it changed from a tortured mushroom color to a soft warm rose.

Epimetheus put on his Titan height. He lifted Pandora down in one hand.

"It isn't your fault, poor Pandora. We've all been tricked. Don't cry."

Music began to play. It was melodious and sweet. It came from out of the Box.

"Slam the lid!" screeched Pandora. She (like the gremlins) hid her face.

But Epimetheus stared, and he said, "The last thing in the Box isn't like the rest."

And a maiden flew up out of the Box, on her shining rainbow wings.

Sitting on the step of the Titan's house, Hope gasped. And so did Cassandra. But it was Miranda who said, in her regal tone, "But Hope—it's *you*."

This was quite true. The maiden who had come from the Box, though winged, was otherwise Hope's double.

"My name is Hope," the winged girl from the Box was saying. "I, too, will go into the world, to help mankind bear its sorrows, but more important, to help mankind to see beyond them."

"But you're only a child," said Epimetheus, gently.

"Only believe in me," said the winged Hope, "and I shall grow."

"Oh, what can *you* do?" snapped Pandora. And with a nasty pride, "I've ruined everything." And for the first time everyone listening wanted to slap her.

But winged Hope answered, "Although the Evils which you let loose, and which now plague humanity, will bring fear and pain, I can lift human hearts above those miseries. You, Pandora, have chained men to the earth with anguish. I will give them wings, on which they can fly away."

And on this grand line, the stage darkened again, and the two pines closed solemnly together. And Augustus and Eli leapt up shouting, "Bravo! Encore!"

But Hope—that is, Hope Glover, the orphaned downstairs maid-of-all-work—she, too, jumped up and she cried, "That's it! Now I know. Give them wings!"

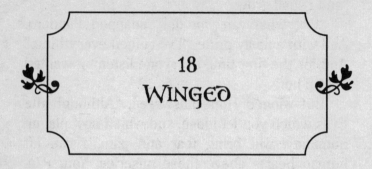

18
WINGED

"It *is* a dream," said Miranda, standing, coolly composed. "But it must be morning now. I can hear the children calling for me."

"And," said Cassandra, "I can hear Edmund bringing me a cup of tea, the dear. But heavens, I'll have to leave right away—" She turned to Sebastian. "Sebastian—good-bye for now. It was wonderful to see you. Do let me know, won't you, if Hope won't mind passing your message on."

"I'm sure she won't."

"Now Edmund's drawing the curtains. He's saying, Wake up Cassandra! Good-bye—"

"And my husband, a cleric, you know," added Miranda, as if forgetting who they were, "he's lost his sermon again. I can hear him turning out the desk drawers. I must go."

And suddenly both Cassandra and Miranda

disappeared, winking out like two candle flames.

But Hope hardly noticed.

She was standing and gazing away across the great open floor, from which everything but the pillars and tiles had faded, now the play was over. Though the Box stood up like solid shadow.

The genie, which had cautiously gotten behind the seats when the Evils flew out, now wafted over to Hope.

"I did quite well...did I?"

"Yes, you did," said Hope, rather vaguely.

But the genie barely reacted. "Your first wish must have put me right. I can't think how."

Hope said, even more vaguely, "Oh, I think I know about that. I was also given a star to wish on, in the palace of King Pegasus—only I didn't. But it must have saved the wish for me, the way *you* did that other time. Anyway, anyway..." She turned to the genie. "I suppose I could wish everything right at once, but I'm not going to risk that. You said magic things don't always take extra magic quite as they ought to—and somehow, I think *I* have to do this. It's my task, the work I've been given. And it's more important than any work I ever had to do."

Behind them, the dwarves were looking in concern up at the gold star which must be the *Basset.* The gremlins had stayed in their hats.

Hope said, "Before anything else, genie, I

must wish that these gentlemen can get back to their ship right away."

"Thank you, Hope," said Malachi. "We'd prefer not to leave her uncrewed too long. The roc may return, a wind may blow up. The air feels stormy."

"Does the banner..." began Hope.

"It still reads VERSED IN COD," grated Archimedes, glowering.

"It was magical, you see," mumbled the genie, "I shouldn't have touched it. At least, not when I was so out of practice."

The dwarves assembled for their magical departure, looking somewhat disapproving. The hatted gremlins were picked up by Captain Malachi, one under each arm.

"Sebastian—wish me luck!" cried Hope.

"No, no, that wish definitely can't work," moaned the genie, but Sebastian only nodded.

"Of course, I do, Hope. All the luck in the Lands of Legend. That's quite an amount."

Then Hope wished the dwarves safely back on the *Basset* and they were gone, and the night seemed larger.

"And now, genie," said Hope.

"Yes, O Mistress of the Lamp-which-isn't-here-but-somewhere-only-where?"

"Wings," said Hope, "I wish for wings."

"Ah," said the genie. It stood on its tail in the

starlight, again looking glum. "I can't."

"Oh, genie! Why can't you? Don't you see, I *have* to have wings."

"Well, of course I don't see, since I don't know your plan of action, O Mistress. But mostly I don't see how I can give you wings. I'll be frank. I *can* work magic on magic things—or once I could—but I haven't the confidence yet. There, that's off my chest. However, the thing about wings is even more complex. You see, it isn't like—say—giving you a different dress, or turning you into something else completely, though I'd be a bit nervous there, too, I confess. No, you see, for example," it waffled on, "I can create an *illusion*—which will look real, but won't *be* real. That is, you'd look as if you had wings—but wouldn't have, and couldn't use them at all, and I feel you want to use them? Otherwise, I *can* bring you real wings—as I so successfully brought the hamper just now, or the chairs (comfortable, weren't they?). And you may recall those woolly doves I brought you by mistake that time—they were part of an enchanter's zoo. The point is, what I bring has to come from somewhere. So if I brought you real *wings* I'd have to remove them first from something else— an owl, say, and the owl would be very fed up, I can assure you—"

Hope didn't know it, but she was dancing from foot to foot in impatience.

The genie interrupted itself. "Wait a minute. I could do it this way—I could turn something *into* wings for you. Preferably something a bit wing-like to begin with."

Hope brightened, looked unsure, then her face cleared completely. "Doves," she said. "Gloves."

She thrust her hand into the pocket of her dress. She pulled out the two little woolly gloves and shook them. She had brought them all this way, and now—

"Gloves," repeated the genie. "I see."

"My mother made them—do you remember? And they *are* like wings," Hope insisted. "Look, they are, and rainbow colored. My mother said they were like wings, she did. Gloves for Hope Glover, she said, like the first Hope's rainbow wings."

"That wasn't saying quite that *they* were like wings."

"Oh, please stop talking and try, genie. You've got all your ability back, I'm sure you have—and this isn't magic on magic even, is it?"

The genie screwed up its face. "Better say the wish again, just to start me off."

So Hope said, "I wish these gloves were my wings and would fly!"

"I hear and obey," bawled the genie, uncertainly.

But something flared bright. Hope was knocked backward and sat down on the hard step from which all the chairs had vanished. The genie coiled up in a ball, and rolled into the hamper, which for some reason was still there.

Then the dazzle was gone.

"Oh, no!"

"Oh dear."

The gloves had indeed become two large glimmering rainbow wings. They were flying around together, batting and flapping, rising up toward the stars, diving toward the ground. Obviously they had the full power of flight. However, they weren't anywhere near Hope.

"I said *my* wings."

"They *are* yours," said the genie. "Just—not attached."

"How can we *attach* them?"

"More difficult now. They're magic now, you see—"

"You said—"

"Yes, but I might make a mistake just from *nerves*, now!"

"Oh, *genie!*"

Hope sprang up again and stamped her foot in frustration, which she'd thought people only did in books.

She had her plan. She felt brave enough to try to make it work. Only soon her courage would leak away, because whatever she did or tried to do, just couldn't seem to work.

A soft tinkling, once, twice, made her look down. There on the giant step, two gold things lay, winking in the starlight. Hope bent and picked them up. They were the E and the D off the *Basset*'s genie-spoilt banner.

"These are magic, too," Hope murmured. "They must be, because the *Basset* is magic. And the dwarves sent them to me, or they came on their own. Oh!" Hope might have turned to stone. Then she came to life again and she said, "If I add an E and a D—"

The genie oozed out of the hamper. "Yes?"

"Get ready, genie. I wish, I wish, I wish—that by adding E and D, I shall be wing*ED!*"

The genie spun on the spot. The two gold letters shot from Hope's hand. They arced through the air like two golden threads, and hit the flying wings with two little bell-like chimes. The E blazed on one wing, the D on the other. Then both letters vanished. The wings vanished. And then Hope felt the strangest sensation, which she could only afterward describe as being like suddenly growing an extra pair of arms *out of her back*. And then she raised these arms and she was gliding up into the air, up and up. Effortlessly the new arms were flexing and waving. They were graceful and strong. Soft light beamed from them and surrounded her. Below her lay, so much smaller now, the giant's floor, the step, and the genie, staring with its cat's eyes, and her own star-cast shadow.

"I'm flying. I'm *flying!*"

Magic *had* worked on magic. Hope was winged.

"I can do anything now! It's meant to happen. *I'm* meant to do it." Hope circled over the sky; she had no fear—perhaps she'd never really be frightened again. Nothing else mattered. She had believed and now she saw the result.

She flitted and swooped like a swallow, and the stars glittered, and she could smell her mother's scent of jasmine. She had had no hope at all. But now she had *become* Hope.

Then the strangest thought occurred to her. *I wish that boy Apollo could see me. Like* this. *I'm not stupid and ignorant now, I'm not useless and a nobody.*" But what on earth did Apollo Rivers matter either? *He'd* helped the centaurs—he was a far bigger fool than she had ever been.

Thunder sounded away in the west. On the wing, Hope turned her head. From so high, she saw great banks of cloud massing threateningly over the sea. Forces were gathering, she could feel it. She soared downward to the mountain, flawlessly. She might have flown all her life.

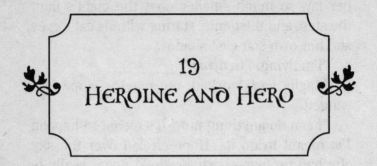

19
HEROINE AND HERO

Was it thunder that woke Apollo? It might have been, or only the guilty feeling he'd had as he fell asleep again after supper with the friendly centaurs in the wood camp. The guilty feeling had stayed in all his dreams, too, so he kept apologizing to dream people. And then, in the last dream, he had seen his father, Mr. Rivers, who had stood puffing at him, "I have a letter here from the horses, Apollo."

"Yes, sir?" Apollo had said uneasily.

"They say they are quite displeased."

"I'm sorry—"

"Speak when you're spoken to. They say that you prefer eating and sleeping in the woods to trying to rescue them from the mines."

"Well no, Father, but—"

"Silence, boy! You spend too much time on

lessons, too much time trying to do all the stupid things I told you that you must." (Apollo gaped.) "You must *daydream,* Apollo. Not to daydream is unforgivable."

"But, Father—"

And then Mr. Rivers opened his mouth and puffed out a cloud of pipe smoke, only it was a thundercloud with lightning in it, and then the thunder boomed—and Apollo woke up.

"That was an odd dream," he said to himself. "Only, for once, Father was right."

It was strange in a way, he thought, how he had come to this conclusion. But also it was as if he had known the truth all along—that magic could be found, that so many of the rules of the ordinary world were not important. He had known, and others had lied to him until he forgot. Now he had been reminded. He would *never* forget again.

Over the night river, lightning still flickered. The second peal of thunder sounded farther off. None of the centaurs, who slept out under the trees in the summer weather, took much notice. A few turned over. One got up and shook himself and lay down again.

Then someone spoke in Apollo's ear and Apollo almost jumped right up a tree.

"Ssh," said the someone.

"What do you mean, giving me a fright like

that and then telling *me* to ssh?"

He saw that Bay, the ginger centaur, was standing there, and behind him two other pale, horsy forms.

"I couldn't sleep," said Bay. "I keep thinking we ought to do something. About those horses in the mines."

"That's right," said one of the pale ones coming forward. It was Quickfoot, Oaken's sister. "We try to be peaceful, to avoid conflict with anyone, but I can't stop thinking either about the roc losing her egg."

"As for myself," said the third figure, in a dignified way, "I owe my loyalty to my own brothers. Though wingless, we, too, are Children of Pegasus, an ancient and noble line." He wasn't a centaur, but Light Mane the white horse.

Then Bay said, "The roc flew away in the end, you know, Thorn told me. She went into the west. She has forceful relatives there, I've heard, a distant cousin or some such. And then again, her egg may have hatched in the mine caves. Klatter's lot will have put it somewhere warm to hurry it on—so, maybe we should all just lie down and go back to—"

"Bay," said Apollo, standing up, "I've had enough of this. You can come, or not. I'm going back to the mountain. I've learned this: the valley centaurs are rude, selfish bullies—but they're idiots. They'll believe anything—even things you just tell them that you've made up—provided they like the sound of it and think it will mean something nice for *them*. I don't see why we shouldn't make fools of them, if we're careful. I'll distract them in some way, flatter them or promise them something. Then Quickfoot and Light Mane can sneak past and set the horses free—in the mines, there should be plenty of chances. As for the roc—we'll have to risk it."

"I didn't know you had a plan," said Bay admiringly.

Apollo, who hadn't, and who had simply invented all he said as he went along, nodded. "Of course. I've been lying here planning for hours."

"What *about* the roc?" said Quickfoot. "She's a mother in distress."

"I'll think of something," lied Apollo.

He felt lighthearted now, glad to be doing something. Perhaps it wouldn't even be all that dangerous.

The wood smelled beautiful by night, and the stars were so bright, especially that one, that huge golden star over there. Tinged by the storm, the air was electric, exciting. This was a true adventure. And for once, Apollo knew without doubt he was trying to do something right.

They went quite fast through the woods,

Apollo running and the others trotting. Among the pines, once they reached them, the going was even easier, as there was less undergrowth. Even so, by the time they came to the outcrops of the mountain, the stars had moved some distance over the sky, and the circling storm seemed to be gathering about the two peaks.

"There's quite an easy path here," said Quickfoot. "I've seen Klatter's band go up this way now and then. They always choose the easiest route."

They began the climb.

Soon the pines fell back. The sky grew ever larger, and above them the storm clouds rumbled. Glancing up, Apollo thought the storm was rather odd, in fact. Banks of cloud crowded across the sky from the west, now and then rippling with lightning. On the peaks of the mountain these clouds looked now nearly solid as the stone. The rest of the sky was clear and starry. But the climb, despite Quickfoot's comment, wasn't entirely easy, and he soon forgot the puzzle.

"This is one of their mine entrances," whispered Quickfoot finally.

"Yes," said Bay, "there's one of their grass baskets."

Apollo peered at the cavelike entry. "Do you know the way, once we're inside, Light Mane?"

"I've never been brought to the mines," said

Light Mane, rather loftily. "They said I was too white to assist in the mining."

Bay, Quickfoot, and Apollo looked at him.

"Er, too *white?*"

"I'd show the dirt more."

Bay sniggered. He sounded just like a horse. Quickfoot quickfootedly kicked him and he lumbered off along the passage. The others followed, and then the dark came down.

"Hang on, I can't see anything," said Apollo.

But the centaurs and Light Mane had perfect night vision, and Apollo, since they wouldn't stop, just had to stay close to them. Then, to his relief, he thought he could see a little after all. And then he saw why. Ahead, where the passage grew narrower, here and there a torch had been stuck in the rockside, and they were alight. It felt close and warm. The thunder was no longer to be heard.

"We must be getting near," whispered Apollo. "Let's go slowly. Bay—*slowly,* I said, and watch out for that—" but Bay had clumsily stumbled on another of the discarded baskets. It toppled and various badly made implements noisily rolled out. Everyone froze, for the mine now echoed hollowly. Then Apollo realized the echo didn't come from Bay and the spilled basket, but from a raucous crowd farther in. Laughter and neighs clearly sounded now, hoots and thumps. Unmistakably, Klatter and the valley centaurs were around the next bend.

"Yes, they're safe enough here, the cowards," said Quickfoot. "The roc couldn't fit in this far. Even the entrance is probably too small for her."

Apollo made up his mind. "Stay here. I'll go on by myself and see what they're doing, and where the horses are."

The centaurs shook their heads, but didn't move. Light Mane simply lowered his noble neck and began to crop some weeds that were growing out of the wall.

Apollo knew he must tread carefully—he was thinking of the first time he had met Klatter. There was a stretch of dark after the last torch, and then red firelight bounced on the walls and roof.

Having reached the turn, Apollo kneeled down, then squinted cautiously around the rock.

It was a familiar scene.

The valley centaurs were having their usual party about the usual smoking bonfire. Cups slopped and clacked, and even from here, which was some way above them, Apollo could smell the sick-making reek of Ivy Brew. Bales of grass lay about, and some of Klatter's centaurs were chomping handfuls. Neigha and Hippo were doing each other's hair, plaiting stone chips and bits of old iron into it. Klatter, Basha, Horso, Hod,

Bod, and Thud were seated quite near the opening of the passage, on a kind of natural platform, and Apollo saw that something was there behind them, on a heap of what looked like chains and mounds of grass and old straw. *They were actually resting their hairy sides on it.* It was the white dome of the roc's egg.

Now Klatter spoke in a loud vain voice.

"That roc, I bet it's off somewhere, fretting."

And all the centaurs on the platform laughed, and the ones lower down, who were eating the grass, neighed and guffawed and stamped and made other ridiculous noises.

"We made a proper fool of it, didn't we?" said Basha.

"Yes. Sticking its great head in at that hole up there, where I told you it would, and me saying, Oh, no, you don't get your egg back till you help us out. Brave as a lion, I was."

"Ho, Klatter. Brave as a lion!"

"Klatter's a lion!"

"Always lion about! Ha ha!"

And Hippo called, "He wasn't when he thought it *could* get in after all, when it started pecking and clawing at the hole and cawing."

Klatter pretended not to notice. He drained his cup and held it out to Basha to refill.

Apollo glanced at another opening up in the opposite wall, which they'd pointed at when all this was said. A wider passage must run in there to this large open cave in the mine. No doubt they'd known the roc could get part of the way through it, and that the wall of stone would stop her getting further. They wanted to show her they had the egg, and tell their terms. Had the roc really understood? Would she come back and agree?

"Here, don't you shove," yapped Horso, flinging at Thud a sudden punch.

"I never shoved. I'll mash your nose for you!" responded Thud.

"It's this egg," said Bod. "It's wriggling."

"Can't be. Eggs don't."

Apollo turned his gaze away. He was searching for a sign of the slave horses. There wasn't one. *They must have penned them somewhere else,* he thought. *Confound it, where?*

Just then Hod plumped forward and almost fell off the platform.

"It *does* wriggle. Gave me a great push."

The centaurs turned and looked at the egg. In the firelight, it shone like a large muddy pearl.

"Do you think—"

"Could it be—"

"Hatching?"

"Just what we planned," said Klatter in a pleased tone, but he stood up and moved a little way off. "A young roc's helpless. Not like the parent bird. We'll soon have it eating out of our hands."

Basha lashed his blond tail and gave his blond mane a good scratch. "I'm not so sure. Hey, Klatter, what do you definitely know about rocs?"

"Knew how to get the egg, didn't I, with that human boy-thing?"

(Apollo grimaced.)

"Yes, but that roc's a big old bird. When it stuck its head in here, you were hiding behind the fire with the rest of us."

Apollo could tell they really hadn't thought their scheme through properly. Meanwhile, he had been staring around the mine cave, past two untidy rusty winching machines and piles of rubbish. It was true, he thought, it looked as if nothing had actually been mined here for ages. The centaurs just liked making the horses carry rubble, to show who was superior. But then he saw how the passage where he was concealed ran down into the cave in natural steps. Just below, going in under these steps, a kind of storage area had been quarried. Apollo thought he could hear something moving in it—the horses. He lay flat and inched forward, and then he was able to peer over one side. Sure enough, the centaurs' horse slaves were there below, jostling a little in the small space. It was dark in there, too. Apollo would have liked to call to them, but exactly then the row in the cave broke off, as Klatter hit Basha on the head with an iron cup. Basha's four horse legs folded and with a grunt he sat down.

In the silence that followed there came a crash of thunder loud enough to shake, let alone be heard in, the inside of the mine.

Hippo shrieked, "It's the roc again!"

All the centaurs (except for Basha, who still sat there shaking his mane) rushed for cover. There were shrill neighs, collisions, and curses, and things fell over, including centaurs and one of the winches. During this upheaval, Apollo leaned down and called in to the horses—but now of course they didn't hear him. They, too, were shifting in a panicky way. A sort of wooden half door closed them in, and one or two kicked at it nervously.

Once this racket dies down, Apollo thought, *I'd better just go out and start bluffing. Say I've got some news or something. Or should I go back and get Bay and Quickfoot? They won't be able to get down the steps without being seen...*

The thunder was dying in deep waves. Silence had come back. And then the quavering voice of Hippo rose from the shadows beyond the fire: "Wh-what's *that?*"

Apollo thought they'd seen him. He sprawled

and tried to force himself into the stone floor. Then he realized the centaurs' shaggy heads, even including Basha's now, were turned the other way.

In the hole in the opposite wall, an eerie glow had begun, like the pale light of a candle, but all the time getting stronger.

"It really is the roc!"

"Is it *luminous?"*

"That's its eyes—glaring in the dark—with bloodlust—"

But instead of the roc's smell, there came the sweet scent of jasmine. And then the hole was completely full of light, and it wasn't a frightening light at all. It was every color at once, shimmering like a shell. And then, wrapped in the light, the light's source, in through the hole in the stone came fluttering a winged being. It wasn't the roc. Nothing like her.

What a wonderful-looking girl! thought Apollo. *Of course, she's got wings, so she must be a fairy. A flower fairy, she smells so nice. Quite a tall one, though—she's nearly as tall as I am. Classical Greek dress, and everything all rainbows from those terrific wings. Oh, good Lord.* Confound it! *It's that rotten little pest Hope Glover!*

The centaurs, however, didn't know anything about any Hope Glover. They simply saw a creature in an aura of shimmering light, and with rainbow wings, hovering there in front of them. They were impressed.

"Who's that?" they asked one another.

"It's a *goddess*," breathed Basha, who was still rather stunned.

Then the creature spoke to them in a bell-like silver voice.

"My name is Hope," announced the winged girl. "I come from Pandora's Box." And then she looked at them quite sternly. "Have you heard of the Box of Pandora?"

Well, I certainly like her cheek, thought Apollo, irritably. Then he couldn't help thinking he did rather like it, too. Hope Glover looked astounding. And how had she got *wings?* And where did she learn to talk like that—she sounded just like—well, like what Basha had said. A goddess, only a very small one.

The centaurs all seemed to think so, too.

Klatter was shouldering forward. Then Horso elbowed him out of the way.

"Your goddesship," said Horso pompously, "we do know about Pandora's Box. We know it's up on the mountain, too, and the roc made a nest in it, pleasing your goddesship."

"We dealt with that roc," said Klatter, elbowing Horso out of the way now. "We stole its egg. Egg's ours. We have a great war to make," elaborated Klatter, even more pompous than Horso, more dramatic than Hope, "a great war with the winged horse things. To show 'em we're best."

"Of course you are," said Hope. "Everyone knows of the famous centaurs, their wisdom, bravery, and skill."

The centaurs, who were still emerging from hiding, with bits of grass and cobwebs in their hair and smudged faces where they had fallen in the soot of the fire, leered cheerfully and agreed.

Apollo thought, *Just what's her game? Now that she's gone magical, she's not going to try to help* them, *is she? Just like a girl, to get everything wrong—*

"You see," said Hope, floating there like a butterfly, "you are to be rewarded for your cleverness and courage."

"How? How? What do we get? How valuable is it?" gobbled the centaurs, pressing around the aura of Hope.

Hope looked down at them. She was smiling, because she was enjoying this very much, and in a strange way its danger was all part of the adventure. She knew she was doing well, too. She had practiced so often, but never with an audience. On the other hand, she really must convince the centaurs totally. Under other circumstances they would have terrified her, their hairy smelly roughness and huge clumping

hooves, their thick-skinned faces that managed
to look comically silly and cruel all at once. She
knew what they were like from the myths, and
also from the talk in the palace of Pegasus. She
understood that if she hadn't looked as she did,
hadn't been winged and seemingly supernatural,
and hadn't spoken with such authority—if she
had been, in other words, just the little girl Hope
Glover—they'd probably have trampled her
underfoot. She had no intention of letting her dis-
guise slip.

She proclaimed, "I came last from Pandora's
Box, to bring hope to the world."

"Yes, yes, quite right—but what's it worth to
us?"

"I am to offer you a great prize," said Hope.
"If you accept it, you will have no more need of
the roc or her egg. You will be able to ascend to
the cloud islands at your own will. Your power
will be extraordinary. No one will be able to stand
against you. You can conquer not only the
winged horses—but the world."

The centaurs snorted and pranced.

Hoofy tried a somersault and fell over Bytis.

Only Basha burbled, "But how?"

"You are to be given the gift of flight," said
Hope. "You are to be given wings."

Now the centaurs were leaping and prancing.

More things got knocked over and some tails went in the fire and had to be put out with howls and whinnyings.

When the noise died away again, Hope came fluttering down and alighted, effortlessly, on a winch. (*She might have been flying about all her life,* thought Apollo, between disgust and admiration.)

"To gain your wings there remains one last test of your bravery," she said. "But I know you are fearless. You are centaurs!"

Apollo made himself stop watching Hope. He eased over the side of the stair and let himself drop down by the wooden door of the horse pen. No one had been looking his way; Hope had provided the perfect distraction. The horses eyed him, pawing the straw inside the enclosure. But Apollo had never been afraid of horses. He let himself into the pen, pushing the door closed behind him. Inside it was very dark.

Outside, he could hear Hope telling the centaurs whatever it was they had to do in order to gain wings for themselves. Was she mad? Apollo moved quietly through the horses, murmuring and stroking them into calm. "There, I'll get you out. Light Mane's waiting, and two centaurs who are kind, from the wood. You'll soon be free, and I'll make sure you stay that way. Do any of you talk?" Someone said falteringly out of the gloom, "Most of us have forgotten how—to speak."

"That's dreadful."

"In the valley—they beat us—if we talked."

Apollo thought of school. "I know what you mean. But *you* haven't forgotten. Who are you?"

"I forget my name."

"Here you are. You've got a fine coat. You're black as cherry-wood boot polish, I could hardly see you in here."

Outside there was yet more bounding and horsy trumpetings, and a great bang and clatter of hooves.

"I don't know what that girl's doing, but I think she's going to get them to go outside from the sound of it. And I think they will. Then we'll make our move."

Hope, standing on the winch, had indeed just told the centaurs they must come out onto the mountain and up to the ruin of the Titan's house. But alarmed, they were disagreeing, insisting the roc might return.

Hope privately refused to think of the roc, though that was now quite difficult. She had in fact found the way through the mountain to the centaurs' lair by following the *smell* of the roc, which still lingered strongly in those passages the bird had been able to push through.

Hope regarded the centaurs very sadly.

"Has your famous courage deserted you? This is a test of your valor. I can make you mightier than the roc. Don't you dare?"

I do wish they'd hurry up, she thought, as they bickered and ran about. Then Klatter surged out of the general mass. "I'll do it. I want wings. Any being who has two qualities is better than one that doesn't. That's why a centaur is superior to men or horses. But give him wings, too—that's three qualities—*unbeatable!*"

"Valiant Klatter," cried Hope, "your fame will be written in the stars."

"And mine," snarled Bytis. "I'll go, too."

Then they were all saying they'd go, and Hippo and Neigha and the rest of the female centaurs were barging up, claiming they were braver than the male centaurs anyway.

There was another passage that wound out of the cave. It was broader than the others—though the centaurs had blocked it with rubble against the roc, just in case. Higher up, it opened out widely. It was the way by which they had brought the egg.

Now they cleared the barricade, and squashed into the passage in a herd. Hope flew over them, encouraging and giving light.

Apollo, looking over the half door, saw all this, and watched Hope and the centaurs vanish. Then he pushed the door wide.

"Come on, horses. It'll be simple now."

But as he stepped out, with the black talking horse beside him, the oddest sound went through the cave.

A twig in the fire, perhaps? It had sounded like that, a bit.

Apollo couldn't help it. He turned and looked up at the deserted platform where the dome of the roc's egg stood on its nest of iron and straw. Then Apollo said something that, if his father or Mr. Ruff had heard it, would have earned him another caning.

Up the side of the white dome, clearly visible in the firelight, ran a black branching crack. And even as Apollo stared at it, another crack ran up, and another. After which one whole piece of the shell, as big as a dinner table, peeled off and dropped away. Out of the gap came thrusting a sharp yellow beak, nearly as long as Apollo was tall, and then the flash of a red-black eye. The junior roc had hatched.

20
THE CENTAURS REWARDED

Eventually the sloping passage came to an end. Hope flew out ahead of the centaurs onto a ledge of the mountain.

Directly below lay the sweeping tiled floor and the empty Box. There was still no sign of the roc, but the storm was growling on the mountain-tops. Hope looked up and in a firework of lightning saw the huge shape of a bird—her heart seemed to stop. Then she realized the bird was only some curious formation of the clouds. And yet, clouds here were different. And hadn't she seen something like this before, in the hour she arrived, a monstrous cloud bird in the storm?

But the centaurs were thrusting and jostling at the mouth of the passage.

"All clear? Is it safe?"

"Fear nothing," cried Hope.

215

"Told you that old roc wouldn't come back," said Klatter, who hadn't said anything of the sort. "And even if it comes it won't attack, with the egg below." He was very brave now, his thoughts obviously filled by wings. He pushed into the open. The others followed.

They got down from the ledges of the mountain to the giant's ruin in a noisy, slithering jumble, the lightning quickening overhead. (Was something up there watching?) Hope, of course, merely flew.

Once everyone was on the tiled floor, glaring up at the great carved Box, another silence fell.

Lightning ebbed and flowed. The tiles gleamed and shadowed and the Box went white and then jet black.

"I don't like the look of it."

"Never did like it, roc or not."

"All the Horrors of the world came out of it," declared Hippo.

Thud seriously announced, "Yes, all the worst things. Hard-Work and Getting-Up-Early and Patience and Not-Losing-Your-Temper and Politeness—rotten awful things."

"And Sharing-Supper—" "And Waiting-Your-Turn—"

"And Washing-Your-Mane," added Neigha with a shudder of true fear.

Hope blinked. Then she said, "It's a fact, the

Miseries of the world escaped the Box, but then, I left the Box as well. It was—oh, it was perfectly all right in there."

"But was it nice?" asked Hippo curiously.

"No," said Basha, "it wasn't. And we know, because didn't we already climb up the side to get that egg. Almost to the top we went, on our grass ropes, and then threw the net and yanked the egg out. Very skilled work, that, not damaging the shell and all—hanging off those ropes and balancing the egg—should have got a medal, *I* say."

Hope improvised quickly. "But you'd never have seen the wonders of the Box from *outside*. They're enchanted so that no one can. It's only if you enter the Box that you find the wonderful things it contains. It's because it *is* so wonderful that everything which comes out of the Box, even the bad things, has wings."

"Here, are you saying—" started Basha.

"Are you saying, to get wings, we have to—" said Bod.

"Go in the *Box?*" finished Klatter.

"Of course," said Hope lightly. "How else?"

"I'm not going in a box!" yapped Basha.

All the centaurs began to yap the same.

Lightning flamed, thunder roared. Hope was aware of a terrifying something in the air above, some presence pressing in on them. *The roc—is it?* she thought. *Oh, I must be quick—*

"But the Box," said Hope in a kind, offhand sort of way, "is full of the most delightful pleasures. I was, myself, so sorry to leave it."

"Delightful *what?*"

"Delicious foods, exciting drinks, the softest beds—"

"Any grass?" demanded Basha.

"Ivy Brew?" shouted several voices.

"Of course, grass. Grass and Ivy Brew everywhere. And the taste was beyond description."

The centaurs stood there, staring up at her in the stormlight, stupid, greedy—and not moving an inch. Then Hope knew there was nothing else for it. She trembled a second but there was no time for trembling. She spread her wings very wide, like a smile. "Dear, glorious centaurs—let me show you the joys of Pandora's Box. I can't tell you, between ourselves, how much I've missed being in there. Nothing out here compares. I think I'll fly quickly in now. Just a few minutes. Or I might be a few hours...years..."

"Hey, don't you go off yet."

But Hope was flying swiftly up to the top of the Box. She flitted onto the highest piece of carving, and risked a look inside.

The interior was still flavored strongly by roc. It was full of straw and dead leaves and other things that might be in a bird's nest, only on a large scale—for example, several whole boughs of trees were there instead of a few twigs. Through and under the nest she could see nothing. But then, magic could be invisible. She was too afraid to look up at the sky.

"Come now, centaurs," called Hope merrily. "Climb up. Use the carvings for hand- and hoof-holds. You'll be able to *fly* down. I'll be inside, if you want me—how lovely to go back in—*whee!*" And Hope flipped up in the air and next dived out of sight, down into Pandora's Box.

"She's got away—hurry—after her!"

The centaurs, too, had decided. They saw the chance of flight slipping from them and began to push and shove and then to heave themselves up the sides of the Box, using some grass ropes still hanging there, the carvings, or grabbing each others' trailing tails—with much swearing and exchanging of blows.

Already well in among the scratchy reeking straw, in a darkness lit fitfully by flicks of lightning, Hope was floundering unseen.

But soon she heard the first centaur come hoofing and scrabbling over the wooden lip and tipping headlong into the nest, which broke his fall.

"Lot of straw in here," she heard him say, apparently eating some.

Another centaur thudded in. Both centaurs at

once began or continued to fight.

Hope wriggled frantically away. She struggled with the straw and pieces of bough for ages, it seemed to her, until she met the side of the Box. And now what? She could feel she was sinking, too, the nest giving way as now centaur after centaur thumped into it with kicks and curses and neighs. Her problem was how to get out again without being seen.

And then all the luck Sebastian had wished Hope came to help her, all the luck in the Lands of Legend.

She saw a flare of lightning, not from above, but nearly in front of her. She clawed through more branches, and there was an opening, a doorway, easily big enough for one small girl with wings—although certainly not for any hefty hairy centaur. It was the keyhole.

"Winged thing, where are you?" came the muddled yells. There were slidings and bumps, too, as the centaurs tumbled lower and deeper in the subsiding nest. "Where's that winged whatsit?" "Take your hoof out of my ear!" "Mind your filthy tail, you!"

But Hope was through the keyhole and out of the Box again, speeding away like an arrow. And in that very instant, the whole sky broke apart like a black plate that had been smashed.

Something even blacker, and screaming, a

whirlwind on two inky wings, plummeted downward, and the gale of its passing sent Hope into a mad spin. She glimpsed a beak clacking like a pair of shears, two eyes like crashing moons. The roc had returned.

The thunder banged. Then something else banged worse.

Hope had thought only of stranding the centaurs in the Box, out of harm's way. She had forgotten the Box had a lid. But the roc, who had nested there, must have remembered. All this while she had, as Hope had sensed, been watching, watching. Now she had rushed to earth. With her gigantic body she had slammed sidelong against the lid, tilted it and thrown it upward, rammed it home. The Box—was *shut.*

The roc stood on the lid now, her shrieking scissored head raised to the storming sky. Which answered her! As she flapped her wings, the cloud bird flapped the roiling darkness back at her. And as if to salute them both, huge drops of rain like glass globes splashed on the mountain.

Then, the roc *spoke.*

It was an awful voice, rusty, machinelike, yet lawless. "Fools can never leave well alone, so now I have imprisoned them, my new enemies." Standing on the closed lid, she rasped, "So now, *you* come out, my *old* enemy."

Hope, who had been blown to the ground, sat

there, not knowing what to do. And then someone else spoke up.

"Now, O beaked lady, that's hardly fair—"

The genie had been coiled somewhere, hiding itself perhaps. But now it emerged and wavered on its tail in front of the Box. Its eyes looked tearful. "I had no choice but to obey Sinbad, you know. He was then the Master of the Lamp."

The roc lowered her head and pecked suddenly at an itch on one wing. Maybe in the politeness code of a roc this was meaningful, because she said, "Very well. I accept your pleas for mercy."

"Oh—ah—"

"Besides, none of this was your doing. And since my new enemies are now trapped, I must find my precious jewel, my egg."

Hope, too, got up. Again there was no time to be scared. And she had to shout so the roc would hear. "That opening, madam," she called, with a quick curtsy. "The passage has been unblocked and should be wide enough. It leads straight to their mine cave. Your egg's there."

"I trust you don't lie, very small bird," said the roc (looking at Hope distractedly, and presumably seeing only the wings), "for up in the sky above us is the greatest of all birds, the Thunder Bird, who nourishes with rain. It is this being who came back with me to help me punish the horse-men. But he will punish you, if you lie."

"No, it isn't a lie."

"Then, I thank you, very small bird. I wish you one day many eggs of your own."

Hope looked at the genie and shook her head.

The genie muttered, "No, I thought you wouldn't really want that one."

But like a spear the roc was flinging herself at the opening Hope had shown her in the mountain. With a rush she tore into the passage—she sounded like a steam train. Small and large stones showered down. Hope and the genie took cover, under the Box.

There was no noise from the centaurs, even after the rock slide had ended. They had probably sunk all the way down inside by now. What would the Box do to them, anything or nothing? They had been horrible, but did even they deserve to be trapped in all that smothery straw and darkness, forever? With nothing to eat or drink, either, except the straw, nothing to do or think about... Surely this would only make them worse?

The rain stopped. The storm seemed to be folding itself up, and outlined by reappearing stars, the Thunder Bird was preening its wings, spreading them out one by one. And as each wing was spread, the stars vanished again for several miles.

"Genie, I do want to make another wish. You're not too tired? I wish that Pandora's Box be made small."

The genie, which had seemed quite pleased, frowned at her.

"You see," said Hope, "if the Box gets small, I think the centaurs will get small, too. I've learned myself," said Hope grimly, "when you *are* small, you can't usually do much. Not unless you put a lot of effort into something, like tonight. Otherwise, no one takes any notice. So, if they were just little and powerless, couldn't they be set free?"

The genie said, "I can't make the Box small. No, it isn't just that it's magic. It's *Pandora's Box!* It's too mighty, too ancient—even for me."

"But Epimetheus said he could make the Box small," said Hope, baffled.

"Epimetheus said it," replied the genie. "I am not he." This use of grammar sounded pretty final.

Hope folded her arms. What was one more frightful risk? "*Then,* O genie, I wish that Epimetheus were here—at once!"

"Ohhh!" said the genie. Then it added hoarsely, "I hear and obey, O Mistress of the Lamp."

As all this was going on on the surface, the

roc had been rushing through the mountain corridors, having had to land and close her wings
and run, which she did rather like a terrifying
chicken. But as Hope had promised, it was possible for the roc to get all the way through,
although with some difficulty here and there,
until the way opened wide before her. Here she
needed only to step over the debris that the centaurs had removed. She was in the heart of their
mine, in the big cave, but it was by now dark. The
bonfire, which had been burning, was nearly out.
And that was because a lot of wet eggshell had
recently dropped into it.

The roc fanned her wings, however, and the
fire gasped out a little red light. The roc uttered
an awesome screech.

Her cry was answered by many others.

In the mine had been a very strange scene
already, but now it was even more peculiar. And
as if appreciating that, the fire burned more
brightly still, to show everything.

What had happened was this. While Hope
and the centaurs had been tumbling about in the
Box, the egg of the roc had hatched.

It did so to a chorus of frightened horse
neighs and the wails of Quickfoot and Bay—who
had come running bravely into the cave on hearing the neighing. Light Mane, who also ran in,
was giving a bleating noise.

Apollo was standing there holding on to the nameless dark talking horse. Perhaps their contact was what kept these two alone from yelling and crying.

Having cracked all over, the egg simply seemed to explode. Shell hailed in all directions, into the fire, half putting it out, against the walls, among the horses. One piece grazed Bay's side and distressed him further. Another piece landed on Apollo's head, and looked like an extremely unsuitable hat.

But no one really noticed that, because the young roc was by now staggering forward out of the remains of its egg.

It was gawky and covered in damp down, like a chick—but it smelled like three hundred full-grown chickens, and was, Apollo thought, unbelievably ugly. Worse than ugly, though, its beak was already like a knife, its eyes were bright, and it was about the size of a very large elephant.

Apollo found he had sat down. He must have turned his foot on a stone.

The baby roc instantly came lunging for him.

Bay snorted. He dashed forward, and Quick-foot, too. But halfway there they halted again—the baby was so enormous.

Only the dark horse stayed by Apollo.

"I know," said Apollo, through his chattering

teeth, "it's making such a horrible noise. It's—hungry—I expect—"

The monster bird lumbered on. It kept giving a kind of rasping clucking sound. Its vast beak, Apollo's own height, dipped swaying toward him.

"*Run,* horse," he croaked, "get away while it tears me in bits—"

"I think it's crying," said the dark horse.

"I know, it's because it's h-hungry—"

"Just confused."

"Please, horse, I'm all right, do run away."

"I remembered my name just now," remarked the dark horse. "Raven. How do you do?" And then it walked quietly up to the baby roc, and gazing up at it from black eyes, the horse called Raven gave a gentle whinny.

The roc baby looked right down. Now it would kill the horse. Apollo jumped to his feet and pelted straight at the roc baby, and the next thing he knew was that he and the horse were spilled over together and the baby roc seemed to be sitting on them. Only it wasn't, and it was—*cooing.*

"There, it was only afraid," said Raven, as the baby nuzzled him. It had its other wing over Apollo, and now it was nuzzling him, too. Its smell was very strong, but there was something fresh about it, too, it was so young, and it was gurgling now, almost like a human baby, sitting there and waggling gigantic yellow bird feet.

"The poor little thing," said Quickfoot, who had also come close, and was stroking its neck, which it bent right down so she could. And Bay was there, saying, in a shaky tone, "Um—coochy-coo—um, diddums."

Light Mane and the other horses had also drifted over. The baby opened its wings wider and wider, nuzzling the horses, and the two centaurs, and Apollo (who rather wished it wouldn't, but it was better than being eaten).

"It wants its mother," he said.

The fire was sinking at that point, and there they were, all of them, all cuddled up with the baby roc.

"Of *course* it wants its mother," said Quickfoot, feeding the baby the flowers from her hair. "Nothing can replace a mother."

And then Mother arrived.

When the screeching and screaming ended, the roc stared at her precious jewel, her baby, hatched and cuddled with horses and centaurs and a human boy. She raised her wings and arched her neck. The roc was seldom much of a talker. The way she had spoken outside was unusual. But the cry she gave now was partly relief and partly shock, and partly a savage jealousy. The baby only heard, as Quickfoot later put it, dabbing her eyes, "His mother's voice."

Everyone got knocked over again as the junior roc bundled through the bonfire, entirely putting it out, and into the wings of his anxious parent.

And it was then that, outside, up on the floor of the giant's house, a shadow fell that was, Hope thought, bigger than the mountain.

The voice of Epimetheus the Titan was so vast, they heard it only as you might hear the wind, or the rush of some colossal waterfall.

"Why have you called me from so far away?"

And Hope, who had done so well, now spoke in a quaky voice worse than the genie's.

"Excuse me, sir. But that Box of yours—the one Pandora opened—do you see, over there?"

"That? Why, so it is. Something was in it once. I can't recall what. So long ago."

"Would you mind shrinking the Box?"

Epimetheus turned his bronzy head. The stars, which were reappearing now in scatterings, seemed to sit on his shoulders. "If you want. Who are you? I can't really see you. Winged...a hummingbird, perhaps, or a bee? Never mind. If it will make you content."

Epimetheus was still kind. He didn't mind being dragged here by a spell or a wish, or granting the request of a bird or bee so small he could hardly make it out. He was evidently great in more than stature.

He leaned right over—it was as if the sky leaned over. He breathed softly on the Box, and a stiff breeze blew—which had the slight scent of mint and peaches, so he must have been eating them, in some gigantic version. The Box, though, seemed to sink inward, but it was only growing smaller, smaller, smaller. In perhaps ten seconds, it lay on the tiles, only the size of a small wardrobe.

"If anything were still in it, would that have shrunk, too?"

"Oh, yes, bee. Shrunk a great deal, although in proportion to its original size. *Was* something in it?"

"Something bad," said Hope.

"Yes, I seem to remember that," said Epimetheus thoughtfully. "I believed it was too late to put it right. Are you glad, bee?"

"Yes, very glad, thank you."

"Then good night. May you have honey."

And Epimetheus took a single step and the night parted like two curtains, and he was gone.

"Genie," said Hope, not pausing to get over Epimetheus (who, as she later said, she never *did* get over, quite), "I wish you to let out the centaurs."

"I hear and obey. There. It's done."

"Is it? Where are they? What's that squeak-ing? Oh!"

Klatter and his band were galloping all over the tiled floor. Their furious neighs and oaths came up like the tiny voices of very little mice. They *were* about mouse size, almost. Frankly, about half mouse size. Almost.

"There's Klatter. I nearly trod on him—"

Klatter never heard. Hope's voice was now too big, as the voice of the Titan had nearly been for her, to hear. He seemed not to see her, either. None of them did. When Hope and the genie began to gather them up, they bit and kicked and swore, but it amounted to very little. Hope and the genie were still busy catching them, however (particularly Klatter kept getting away), when the procession came out of the mountain above.

First appeared a tall thin boy and a dark horse, both with black eyes. They looked about, then stood aside. "The centaurs have gone. That girl's taken them off somewhere," said the boy, contemptuously.

Hope pulled a face. He hadn't seen her yet, but she knew *him*. It was that beast, Apollo Rivers. How dare he? And why was he wearing that stupid hat?

But then a herd of horses trotted out of the mountainside, and then two centaurs that Hope could see at once weren't like the others. Last came the most astonishing sight. It was the roc, but she was quite calm, strutting rather than flying, one sooty wing extended over a funny awkward *huge baby* roc—Hope recognized it instantly from an illustration she had seen years before in the *Arabian Nights*.

The mother roc stopped on the ledge, and turned to Apollo. She made a typical roc sound, and everyone jumped. Then they heard her clear her throat. She found words.

"There's no quarrel between us, man-boy. And no longer any quarrel between my kind and the horse kind, whether they are winged or not. All of you acted well to my hatchling. You comforted him and kept him warm, and this centaur lady fed him blue flowers, which will be good for him. Besides, he likes you. We are friends."

Apollo made a most dashing bow. The bit of shell fell off his head. Hope giggled, angry because, for a split second, she had admired him.

"Noble madam, you do us great honor," cried Apollo theatrically.

But the roc only inclined her head, and now took hold of her feathery child by the back of his neck, just the way a mother cat does with her kitten, and the young roc looked perfectly happy about this. Then she flew up into the night sky with him, where the last of the storm clouds enfolded her in an affectionate way. They were gone.

As the horses, centaurs, and Apollo started down toward the floor, Hope flew up suddenly and flapped in their faces with fussy rainbow wings. Horses reared, Quickfoot screamed, Apollo cursed.

"I might have known it would be you, you pest, Hope Glover. Just because you've put on wings and got friendly with those disgusting centaurs from the valley—"

"*I've* got friendly with them! You're the one that helped them steal the roc's egg."

"Well. That was a mistake. Anyway, what's your excuse, you wretched girl?"

"Excuse? I won't make any excuses to *you*. It's the last time you'll ever give me orders or upset me. *I* have taken care of the centaurs. They've been in Pandora's Box and now they're tiny. They couldn't hurt a fly—well, only just. So mind where you're putting your big feet, you *boy*. *Don't tread on Klatter!*"

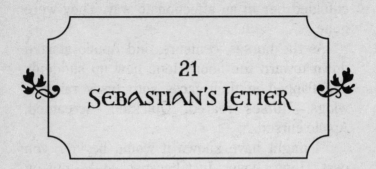

21
Sebastian's Letter

What happened after that can be told fairly quickly, for though it took several days, they were so full, they seemed to pass in a flash.

First of all, Hope and Apollo parted on bad terms, but each said, "Who cares? So there." Apollo was given the gift of a ride by Raven, swung up on the horse's back, and he and the rest of the herd, with the centaurs Bay and Quickfoot, picked a careful way down from the mountain and back into the pine forest. Here they met with the other centaurs from the wood camp, who after all were coming to look for them and help in the rescue. Apollo showed the wood centaurs the present they'd brought for the centaur foal-children.

Once they reached the camp by the river, no one attempted to go back to sleep. They had a party until dawn, with reed pipes playing and little drums beating, while tiny fairies, attracted by the songs, came and perched in the trees, lighting them like miniature lamps, because fairies, of course, are able to glow in the dark.

The foals were delighted with their new pets. "You must be very kind to them, and look after them. Wash and groom them every day, and feed them regularly—or you can't keep them," said Quickfoot firmly. But she knew well the foals were always trustworthy and loving to their pets. In fact, they set about making the pets a pen, at once, and it was finished before everyone did finally go to bed. The pen was about two feet high and ten feet square, made of strong twigs woven together and lined by soft ferns and clover. If you looked in, you could just see the squeaking centaurs of Klatter's band cantering about, punching each other and falling over. How they had hated being washed and tidied.

"And be careful," Quickfoot had warned, "they bite." But really the bites were hardly to be felt. "I hope their characters improve," said Quickfoot. She thought they probably wouldn't.

Meanwhile Hope and the genie went up and up through the night sky, and as they were doing this, Hope turned on the wing, and saw a sight she would never forget. A figure was standing up out of the sea, and on his arm had settled a bird,

which he seemed to be feeding with something
that he plucked from the sky. The figure, of
course, was gigantic, and so was the bird, or
Hope couldn't have seen them. Epimetheus, at
the far horizon, was feeding the roc with drips of
sweet starlight, which must have hardened there
in luminous lollipops. Then the image faded away
like a dream.

There was a great golden star to Hope's right.
It was the *Basset,* and Hope and the genie sprang
in over her side.

"Oh, look at the banner—"

There it stretched, fluttering a little in the
night breeze, and it was almost right, reading
now CREDENDO VI S.

Archimedes stood at the helm. He lifted one
hand. Eli crossed the deck. "Well done, Hope.
You look as if you've had a success."

"I have! And I couldn't have done it without
the letters off the banner. But now I'd better give
them back, hadn't I? How I shall miss being
winged. If only there was a way to—but obviously, there isn't."

So flight had to go. The genie bustled to the
task, and the wings disappeared with far less fuss
than they had arrived. Hope couldn't help her
face falling, besides which she felt very unbal-
anced for a while. But then she fished in her
pocket and there were the two little knitted baby

gloves, just as they had always been, too small and rather shabby. No one could ever guess what they had been and what they had done, and this seemed extra sad. But then Hope put them to her cheek, and smelled the scent of jasmine. Her mother had made them, that hadn't changed. That was what really mattered.

And a quiet cheer was rising on the deck of the *Basset*. Hope looked up in time to see the gold E and D twirling in the air and then attaching themselves to the ship's banner. And you had to admit, that *did* look exactly as it should.

CREDENDO VIDES, the banner read.

Believing is seeing.

All the dwarves were there by then, and Hope hugged them all (they *hrumphed* a little), but especially she hugged Sebastian, who didn't *hrumph* at all. Hugging, in fact, was a lot easier *without* wings. As for the genie, a horde of gremlins had appeared, looking very solemn (which the dwarves assured Hope was most unusual). The balance of magic on the ship had been disturbed by the genie's mishaps, Augustus murmured, and for this reason the gremlins, always spontaneous, had hidden its lamp. Also perhaps because *they* were the makers of chaos aboard. It was their "job" and no one else's. But Augustus wouldn't be quite definite there. Now, however, the gremlins returned the lamp, tipping it out on the deck from a particularly wriggly, bulging black hat.

"Just look, they've cleaned it, too," said the genie, clearly pleased. The lamp shone like mirror. Sebastian told Hope it was more likely the genie's recovery of its talents that had polished the lamp. But now the gremlins were going mad, scampering about and swinging on the rigging, and as Eli observed, it was much too late to go to bed, so they had a party until dawn, when it would be—as Sebastian pointed out—just a very early bedtime.

That night the genie had sent a message to the court of Pegasus. The next few days brought visits to the islands of cloud, and the thanks of Pegasus and his Queen. Another unforgettable sight for Hope was the image of Black Grass drifting gracefully through the air on the updrafts of her husband's white wings. Then came a feast of many days and nights, at which Hope and Apollo—to both their horror on seeing the other—were the guests of honor. The King and Queen gave them many gifts, amazing things, such as sunlight in a bottle and starshine made into a silk cravat. When either received praise or a reward, the other one would clap with a face like thunder.

Every time Hope and Apollo met, when alone, they were cuttingly sharp and rude to each other.

But the strange thing was, they kept meeting. It was as if they were seeking each other out, just for the joy of being nasty. Even belowdecks on the *Basset,* which the dwarves, to Hope's dismay, had invited Apollo to visit, they somehow never managed to avoid each other. Dressed in fantastic clothes from the ship's closets, they would meet in the undersea saloon (stared at by passing mermaids) or the library (stared at by some of the books which had eyes) and in endless corridors full of curios that all seemed to be staring. And here Hope and Apollo would fling insults until one or the other stalked off. Finally one of the arguments got to—somehow—the fashionable dances of London. And in order to show each other up, they went into the splendid ballroom within the *Basset,* and danced the polka together. They insulted each other relentlessly all the way through, but then began laughing. Then they laughed so much they sat on the floor.

"I say, Hope, let's shake hands and be friends, can't we? I'll admit it, I was a useless beast, but I'm better now, aren't I? I will say you're worth— well, *ten* of me, because now I know from the dwarves and everyone what you really did here. The way you stood up to those valley centaurs—I didn't—and you fooled the lot of them and stopped them for good. You're a true heroine. And after the rotten life you must have had at home—I mean back there, in my father's house."

Then Hope said, "I never knew there was anything worthwhile left, and no kindness, not until I met Cassandra and Sebastian and came here, and found all this magic and beauty because of the *Basset*. Then I woke up. But you must have had a nasty time, too, to make you so horrible. Because you're not horrible at all. You're brave—the roc baby, and Sebastian told me about the horses—and funny—and a perfect gentleman! And you can *ride* properly. I wish you'd teach me to ride—after the winged horses I'll miss it so—"

"I will! I will, Hope, I promise. I'll teach you anything they teach me that you want to learn. Even Latin. Though I'm not very good at it."

"But isn't it terrible, Apollo? Tomorrow all the feasts and parties end. And we'll have to go back, won't we? I mean...to London. I asked Sebastian and Captain Malachi. They were very kind, but they said they thought I would have to."

"I asked the captain, too. He tells such marvelous stories about this place. But yes, he said I'd—we'd—have to go back. Our ordinary lives are there, you see. This place—is for our dreams. Our *true* dreams."

"Then—what shall we do?" asked Hope wretchedly. "Oh—all those people—they'll make us go back to being stupid and cruel—and afraid!"

Apollo stood up very straight. "We've seen all this, though, now. We've seen winged horses and centaurs, fairies and giants, and rocs and genii. We've seen the *Basset* and she's *real*. They're all real. After this, what does Cavalry Square, or school, or any of that matter? We're different. We've changed. We've done things most of *them* never could. And just think, in a few years we'll be grown up. Until then, we'll stand by each other. I'll protect you, somehow I will, from those horrors—my father and mother, Mrs. Crackle the cook—all of them. And you must swear you'll protect me from turning back into a beast."

The last hours were going so fast. Now, together, they explored the *Basset,* for what was, probably, the last time. Although the *Basset,* they decided, was in the end too big to be entirely explored, even if you had seven years to do it.

The very final evening was terribly sad for them. Waved off by horse wings, the Wuntarlabe pointed down and west, and the *Basset* left the sky and sank, like a golden planet, into the ocean. She set sail toward the sunset. Above, the islands of cloud seemed to be dissolving into the rosy air, coming unanchored even, drifting away. Centaurs waved their hands from the beaches of the mountain island, and the horses ran and played in the sand, all of them talking now that they were free and their names remembered, Raven and Swan, Light Mane and Fountain Tail and Flame Flanks, and even the shyest ones called Squirrel or Copper or Daisy.

Two knitted rainbow doves, the ones the genie had brought by error from an enchanter's zoo, had been seen flying in the forest. Apollo, who had climbed up to look, reported they now had a rainbow egg, which also looked knitted. Naturally, he had left the egg alone. His birds-nesting was done.

The genie, too, had set off to tour the Lands of Legend. It used the lamp as a strange sort of whirling craft. "Those gremlins spring cleaned inside, too," it had said to Hope. "Everything's in the wrong place. But I suppose they meant well. On the other hand, I do think the magic's got even stronger from being in their hats. No last wishes?"

"I only wish," said Hope, "I could stay here."

"Here's magic. Won't work."

"But—"

There were no Buts. It was all Good-byes.

"Good-bye, King Pegasus, good-bye Queen Black Grass. Good-bye Perichrysos and Melanippos and Quickfoot, good-bye genie, good-bye Captain Malachi, Eli and Archimedes and Augustus—" So many good-byes. "Oh, Sebastian, good-bye—good-bye—and I don't want to go!"

Apollo was up in the *Basset*'s crow's nest, having a last lookout. Sebastian drew tearful Hope gently along the deck, holding her hand. Tiny fireflies perched on the rails—Apollo had already shown Hope that they were the tiniest fairies, come to see them off.

"You know now that dreams can come true, Hope, and that magic exists. You've made a close, good friend to protect you, one that you must protect, too, in your own world. More than that, you've learned how much courage you have, and how brave and clever you are, and how strong, but best of all, that you are really and truly a wonderful actress."

"Have I? Yes, yes, I have."

"Besides," said Sebastian, "when you go back, there's Cassandra. She said she'd like you to try to meet her at two o'clock, on what will be tomorrow, in the park. I understand from Apollo he'll find a way to see you get there."

"Cassandra!"

"And when you do, will you very kindly give her this letter? We're such old friends, she and I. Yet somehow we never exchanged any token, as friends should. She was a little springtime on the *Basset*. She gave us hope, Hope, concerning the abilities of the human heart."

Hope, not quite understanding, yet stood in awe. Then she took the letter in its envelope which Sebastian held out to her.

"I'll make sure she gets it."

"Thank you. But now, let me tell you something of what was in that letter she sent through you to me."

Then Sebastian explained how Cassandra had described to Sebastian, in her letter, how she and Miranda so often dreamed of the *Basset,* and of being there. But Cassandra had said, Where you went in dreams wasn't real, was it?

"But of course, sometimes it *is* real," said Sebastian. "Which is what I've written to tell her."

"And *I* saw her, too, in her dream, when she came to the Titan's house with Miranda, and we all watched the story of Pandora."

"Which you must tell her, too. But there was one other thing."

"Yes, Sebastian?"

"Cassandra also says in her letter that once before she dreamed of you, after she first met you. It was a dream of the future." Hope's eyes grew very round. Sebastian said, "Cassandra dreamed of being at the theater. Hundreds of people came every night to see the play. And the actress. It was you."

Hope hesitated...

The rose pink sun went down in a hush of silver-gold. The night made the sky and sea into one single endless dark blue space. Through this the *Basset* now sailed on, and nothing else was to be seen but the frilled curve of the little waves that caught the fairy lights from the ship's rails. Until at length the fairies also lifted away, and streamed, like a swarm of spangled bees, back toward those unseen shores behind.

Hope said, after her long, long hesitation, "But it was only a dream…"

"*Credendo vides,* my dear. Always remember. And now, it really must be an early night."

So Hope went down to her cabin on the *Basset,* and Apollo went to his cabin, which looked like something from a pirate story and had a hammock that swung. They both fell asleep very quickly, and slept very well, rocked by the rhythm of the ship and the sea.

What had been complicated now turned out to be appallingly simple. When they woke in the morning, it wasn't morning at all—and they were no longer on the *Basset.* They were wearing their everyday clothes and up in the oak tree of the Riverses' garden, at Number 15, Cavalry Square. They had been gone many, many days and nights, but less than an hour had passed here. Only the magic kite—and Hope's maid's cap— had vanished, like the sunset. Scolding voices shouted for them from below. It was time to come back to earth.

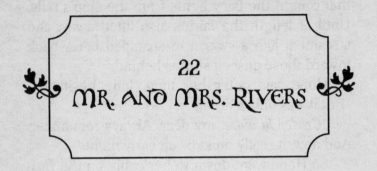

22
MR. AND MRS. RIVERS

The next few years weren't at all easy for Hope or for Apollo. There were many times when they were desperately unhappy, and felt they had reached their wit's end, in that dreadful cramping heartless household in the square. But they had sworn to stand by and to stay true to each other, and they did, and through that and the friendship of Cassandra and Edmund, and because they never doubted that their adventures in the Lands of Legend had been anything but real—they stayed true not only to each other, but to themselves.

Sometimes they were able to meet in the Riverses' garden, up in the boughs of the *Quercus orichalcus,* the Golden Oak through which they had first climbed to the kite.

In the end, they made a new promise to each

other in this tree. Then they did something which caused a great scandal in Cavalry Square—they ran away and got married.

And not long after that, through hard work and good fortune and talent and—most important of all—*belief,* they got the other thing they wanted. So that only seven years after the date at the beginning of this book, in fact in 1874 (when Hope was just eighteen and Apollo not yet twenty-one), they were one of the most famous couples, not only in London, but in Europe.

Cassandra's dream had been quite true. She often thought of it when she went to see her young friend, Mrs. Hope Rivers, take the leading role in a play at Apollo Rivers's own theater, the Dark Horse. For Hope had become one of the great actresses of her day, and her husband one of the most celebrated of London's actor-managers.

Every night, when Hope and Apollo acted, flowers would be thrown onto the stage, so many (it was said) that ten horse-drawn carriages were needed afterward, to carry them all away.

On one particular night, however, late in the spring, when Hope had been acting in a play which told the story of Pandora's Box, she picked up one of the bouquets. She showed it to Apollo afterward in the dressing room, where two little rainbow baby gloves were always pinned on the mirror for luck.

They both stared long and hard.

In the bouquet were some lovely silvery pink flowers, whose petals were the shape of tears, and with these were flowers which weren't flowers at all, but incredibly long, shimmering feathers, white with a sheen like pearls, black with a sheen like sapphires, tawny with a sheen like opals.

"The kind of feathers you might think," said Apollo, "might come from the wings—"

"Of a winged horse!" finished Hope.

Then they heard the commotion in the street, and opening a window, looked out.

There was the normal large theater crowd, but they were shouting and laughing and pointing up at something on top of the theater. Hope and Apollo craned their necks, but because of the angle of the window couldn't quite see far enough.

"I wonder what it is. And these flowers—my dresser says she thought she saw a spectacled, very little gentleman with a long silvery beard, throw them from a box—but no one had hired the box, and it was empty—"

"Do you remember the bottle of sunlight," asked Apollo wistfully, "and the silk cravat made of starshine—"

"We used them both up that time you got caned again and Mrs. Crackle tried to push me in the oven," said Hope.

"But," said Apollo, "they did come through into this world, like Sebastian's letter to Cassandra, and Cassandra's pendant, and Miranda's dress. All those things helped us to believe we never dreamed the *Basset*—"

"Despite waking up in the tree—"

"Despite everything—"

"And this play is about Pandora's Box—"

Then there were screams and applause together from below.

"Look! Look!" they heard people shouting. "What a showman he is, that Apollo Rivers! You'd think it was almost real!"

Hand in hand, Apollo and Hope, Mr. and Mrs. Rivers, gazed up into the smoky spring sky over the city of London. Up there, high above the chimney pots and spires, a white horse, a tawny horse, and a black horse were flying away on moonlit wings. A silence fell, even in the street, and lasted some minutes.

Then, from below, the voice of so-called reality spoke in a loud and determined way. "Pooh. Anyone could see it was only pigeons."

Mr. and Mrs. Rivers looked at each other, and *laughed.*

Always Believe

ABOUT THE AUTHOR

Best-selling author of more than sixty novels and almost two hundred short stories, TANITH LEE is one of today's leading fantasy writers. She has won many awards, including the World Fantasy Award, and her work has been translated around the world.

Born and raised in England, she now lives with her husband on the Sussex Weald, a few miles from the sea.